A DYLAN MAPLES ADVENTURE

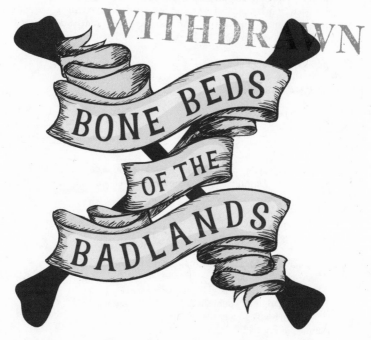

BONE BEDS OF THE BADLANDS

SHANE PEACOCK

NIMBUS
PUBLISHING
NIMBUS.CA

Nimbus Publishing Limited
3660 Strawberry Hill Street, Halifax, NS, B3K 5A9
(902) 455-4286 nimbus.ca

Printed and bound in Canada

NB1389

This story is a work of fiction. Names, characters, incidents, and places, including organizations and institutions, either are the product of the author's imagination or are used fictitiously.

Cover design: Cyanotype Books
Interior design: Jenn Embree

Library and Archives Canada Cataloguing in Publication
    Peacock, Shane, author
    Bone beds of the Badlands / Shane Peacock.
    Reprint. Originally published: Toronto: Penguin, 2001.
    "A Dylan Maples adventure."
    Issued in print and electronic formats.
    ISBN 978-1-77108-658-5 (softcover).
    —ISBN 978-1-77108-659-2 (HTML)

I. Title.
PS8581.E234B66 2018   jC813'.54   C2018-902866-1
                                          C2018-902867-X

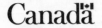 

Nimbus Publishing acknowledges the financial support for its publish-ing activities from the Government of Canada, the Canada Council for the Arts, and from the Province of Nova Scotia. We are pleased to work in partnership with the Province of Nova Scotia to develop and promote our creative industries for the benefit of all Nova Scotians.

JNYS
PEAC

For Sammy,
who knows there's no place like home

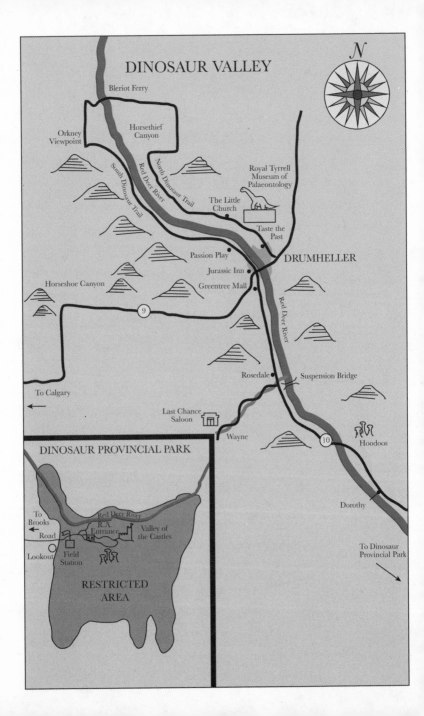

TABLE OF CONTENTS

1. TERRIBLE LIZARD 1

2. DINOSAUR HALL 18

3. A DARK DREAM 37

4. BONES 50

5. A CHANGE OF PLANS 65

6. A REPTILE NEARBY 73

7. WHAT OPHELIA HEARD 93

8. FOOTPRINTS 104

9. LAND OF FEAR 125

10. LOST 137

11. THE FLAG 148

12. HUNTING HIM 157

13. UP CLOSE AND PERSONAL 165

14. A Killer on Our Trail 172

15. The Showdown 184

16. The Evil One 189

1

TERRIBLE LIZARD

*E*arly June, Calgary, Alberta, under a blistering urban sun. A young reporter looks dramatically into a television camera. Behind her, a notorious criminal, convicted of gruesome crimes, emerges from the dark interior of a police cruiser and comes into view. He is led towards a courthouse, handcuffed, his ankles chained.

"He stands seven feet tall," intones the reporter, "and is as thin as a ranch-rail, with a shaved head, pockmarked skin, and piercing eyes. Hear his sensational story at eleven."

The convict shuffles out of the shadows and into the bright glare, his dark eyes becoming slits. The reporter and her cameraman turn and rush towards him. But they and *others are pushed back by a quartet of policemen and burly jail guards. The criminal glances at the gathering media and then focuses his gaze and an unnerving smile on the young woman. She returns his look for a moment but then moves away, her face becoming white.*

Fifteen minutes later she gets a call on her cellphone.

It's him!

"It was nice to meet you," he says in a sickly sweet voice. "I'll look you up some time. Oh, and tell Alberta to have a nice week. Tell them...I'm coming. I'm free!"

Then there was a beep.

It had been his sentencing day and the guards had been rushing him into the courthouse. In the hallway, he had asked to use a washroom. They had taken him to a stark, concrete room with two toilets and a very small window. When they broke down the door five minutes later, they found the guard who had accompanied him lying on the floor, unconscious. Otherwise the room was empty.

The Royal Canadian Mounted Police go on full-scale alert, nationwide bulletins are issued, and Albertans everywhere imagine finding this desperado on their doorsteps.

"The Reptile," the one and only, is loose.

WE WERE SKY-HIGH, LITERALLY. Man, was I having fun. Ten kilometres above Manitoba, all my buds in tow, and the parental units back home in Toronto. It doesn't get much better than that. And to top it all off, we were about to go on a dinosaur hunt.

I'm still not sure how we pulled it off, but me and Bomb Connors, Rhett Norton, and Terry Singh had hit the jackpot—the scientific, paleontological jackpot, that is. We had built a *Tyrannosaurus rex* about half the size of this big baby we were flying to Calgary, and made it actually move and roar and take swipes at people. Then we'd entered it into some science fairs, and before you could say "edmontosaurus," we were national champions and on our way to dinosaur country in the badlands of Alberta.

If the truth were known, our dads almost built the thing for us. At first they said they just wanted to watch, but almost right away they started drawing up all sorts of plans. We could barely even get at our own project! But boy, by the time they were finished with it, it almost seemed like it was alive, and a couple of moms were ready to kill them, T. rex style, because they practically lived in the basement for about two straight months.

First we entered it into the Moore Park Junior High Science Fair, and it just cleaned up there. A little on the spectacular side, one might say, the biggest meat-eating monster the world has ever known, nearly twice the height of your average school principal, coming right into your kitchen. It scared the bejeebers out of most of the girls we knew. For some reason it would give a huge roar and swipe every time they got near it (our sweaty little paws on the on/off switch, of course).

Next was the National Science Fair in Nepean, and it ate up the competition there, too. Not bad for a bunch of grade eights who hate science class. Anyway, they gave us a choice of a trip anywhere in Canada for a week or so as a prize, providing it had some scientific significance to it. We figured we'd built a T. rex, right? Let's go dino hunting!

So, southern Alberta it was. Not exactly the world's most exciting place, I know. Calgary isn't Toronto, and Drumheller, the little town we were headed to, wasn't exactly Vegas, but we knew that scientists had been digging dinosaurs out of the ground in those parts for over a century. It couldn't be totally bad. And besides, all four of us got to go. That was dynamite!

"Sit down, boys, and behave yourselves!" said a whiny voice from across the aisle.

Well, it wasn't all dynamite. That was Newcombe. Norris Newcombe, our science teacher. He and his wife, Ophelia, were our chaperones. And *they* were a royal pain in the butt! But we had plans for them. We were going to give them the slip as soon as we got to Dinosaur Valley, at least for a while.

When you fly into Calgary you get quite a view. There's the city, appearing out of what looks like about a million kilometres of fields and more fields: skyscrapers and subdivisions popping right up out of cattle country. You start seeing some hills, foothills they call them, that look as if they're just bubbling up from all that flatness, and then in the distance you see the Rocky Mountains. Pretty cool, really. I had to admit that there was nothing like that at home.

The airport was just like the whole city. Everything seemed new. In the lobby there were these employees dressed in white shirts, red vests, and big white cowboy hats called Stetsons. And downstairs in the main hall, they had lots of stuffed animals on display, big ones, all from the west. The buffalo kind of caught my eye at first, but then we saw a whole platform filled with dinosaurs. We dropped our bags and sped over. A T. rex, an albertosaurus (just about as vicious but a little smaller and wickedly fast), and a triceratops loomed out over the crowds. On the plaque nearby was information about the Royal Tyrrell Museum, in Drumheller. It said they had discovered thirty-five species of dinosaurs in Alberta, more than they'd found anywhere else in the world.

"Who do you think would win if Alberto-VO5 there faced off against the T-man?" snapped the Bomb.

"T. rex, dude," said Terry. "No contest. Tear his head off at the stem."

"Yeah, but Albert's got the speed, man," cracked Rhett. "He's got the wheels."

"I'll take size and brute strength over speed any day," said Bomber.

"These guys don't often fight each other, you twits," I reminded them, "they're meat-eaters. They're looking for easier kills, veggie munchers, like Tri-boy here, or some big juicy brontosaurus on his last legs."

We hadn't seen Norris easing up behind us. When we did, we could tell by the frown on his face that he had heard us. Uh-oh.

"We aren't here to dredge up the most vicious scenarios we can about these magnificent beasts. All I've heard from you gentlemen since we left is how violent this meat-eater is or how aggressive that one is. Let's try to be a bit more scientific, shall we? By the way, it's apatosaurus, not brontosaurus, and they're Late Jurassic, not Cretaceous—there is no evidence that they ever lived in Alberta. And another thing." He turned and looked over at our bags, sitting alone not far off. "What did I tell you about leaving your bags lying around? And what do they say about every five minutes over the public-address system?"

"Do not leave your bags unattended," I said, trying not to sound as excruciatingly bored as I was. It was the five millionth time he'd made his point.

"Right. Pick them up, boys, and let's find our van."

"Rats," whispered Rhett. "Mad bombers foiled again." Norris had rented a van for us: a big one, almost like a minibus, our touring-mobile. We were itching to come up with a nickname for it. A gross one would have been nice.

We walked by a little magazine store and saw some of the local newspapers sitting out on a rack. It was just a few weeks before school ended back home, so the Calgary Flames had been on vacation for a while—wrong time for hockey news. But the front-page headlines jumped out at me. They were thick and black. "REPTILE ON THE LOOSE!" read one. "DANGER TO US ALL, SAY MOUNTIES!" shouted another. Under each was a picture of this creepy-looking guy with bad skin, dressed in black, a big black Stetson on his head, a snarl on his lips.

Norris picked up a paper and paid for it. I heard him speaking with his wife.

"They say he's heading northeast from Calgary," he almost whispered to her. Then he skimmed the article.

"Oh dear. This guy is a real piece of work. Apparently, he has a thing for bones. Human bones."

As we got closer, he folded the paper under his arm.

"Nothing to see here, boys. I believe our van is at gate seven." He and Ophelia steered us away.

IT TURNED OUT THAT THE VAN was green. We wanted to call it the Snotmobile, but Norris got wind of that almost right away, and after he was finished with us we didn't dare use that word again, even in private. He steered it through the busy streets and pointed out things like the "famous" Glenbow Museum and "historic" Fort Calgary.

They wanted us to see a little of the downtown area before we headed out into the Wild West. My friends got bored with that sort of thing pretty quickly, but I must admit I would have liked to have gone inside all of those buildings. I just love history. It always seems so neat to me that there used to be different people wearing different clothes and thinking in totally different ways, right where we are now. To me, it's like something from a dream. Or from another planet. But I tried not to seem too interested.

Back home in Toronto, they've been putting all sorts of plastic moose on the streets. Our mayor and the other deep-thinking adults who run the place believe Americans think that's kind of cute and very Canadian. It supposedly makes them want to visit the city and spend their money. Well, Calgarians (as they're called) are into that too. Except with them it's cows. We couldn't go more than a few blocks without seeing a plastic moo machine. Whoopee. I don't know if it was the Americans they were trying to impress or not, but they sure went at it. Canadians: we always seem to be trying to impress someone.

There were some pretty cool things about Calgary, too. One of them was the glass walkways between the big buildings downtown. You can stroll a storey or so above the streets just about anywhere. Probably makes sense for a place where the temperature gets down to about five thousand below zero in the winter.

And I just couldn't get over how new everything seemed in Calgary. There wasn't a concrete building in sight. Everything was glass and very tall. We were all craning our necks looking up—not an easy thing to make Toronto kids do. Norris was nice enough to whip by some of the sports places, too...after we pleaded with him. The Saddledome, where the Flames play, was amazing, built like something a giant cowboy would set his butt onto. Actually, it isn't called that now: some company gave the owners big bucks to add their name to it, a name that has nothing to do with hockey. One of these days there'll be a rink called the Ever Ready Underwear Arena or something like that, just so everybody involved can make a few more dollars.

We saw the stadium where the Stampeders play football, and Norris even took us over to the west end of the city to see Olympic Park, where the 1988 Winter Games were. The ski-jump ramps looked pretty awesome—we could just imagine flying through the air off one of those babies.

Before long, Norris was heading the Unmentionable mobile north. We crossed over a few bridges and then got onto Highway 2 in the direction of Edmonton, once home to the mighty Gretzky, and now the Kingdom of Connor McDavid. It didn't take long to get out of Calgary: there were just a few wheat fields and then some suburban towns. Not long after we passed Airdrie, we turned straight east and pointed towards Drumheller. And I mean straight. The road looked as if it had been drawn with a ruler. We were out of the foothills now, and the land was like a pancake. Old Norris was just bombing along the road—they say these flat stretches will make an easterner lose track of speed. We started putting bets on when the RCMP would nail him. We were hoping, anyway. There was a no-cellphones rule, so we had to find other things to do.

There were wheat fields and canola fields stretching out for many kilometres, houses and round metal barns and silos way off the road with clusters of trees around them. The crops were just getting going, sprouting up in different colours as far as your eyes could see. And then we would come upon endless open spaces just filled with sagebrush, like the setting for a Wild West movie. I almost expected to see the Blackfoot Nation appear on horseback on the horizon, or cowboys riding towards us. We even saw a coyote run across the highway in front of the van, as if he were on a mission or something, hunting his prey. It was the real Canadian west. Everything just seemed so big. Even the sky looked bigger out there.

After a while, it began to seem as though the wide-open spaces would never end. Norris was blathering on about how some of these farms had more than five hundred hectares of land and hundreds and hundreds of cattle. He pointed out tractors and farm equipment the size of Mississauga working the fields. All right, all right. Stunning. But let me see a tree or two near the road every now and then, or let the road maybe curve a centimetre, or maybe have a hill in it bigger than a molehill! Let's have some imagination!

Then, without warning, we came upon a part of Canada that looked like Mars. Man, was it wicked! That was the perfect way to describe it. Absolutely wicked. About twenty kilometres out of Drumheller, coming around the first corner we'd taken since we'd left Calgary, we saw what looked like some sort of canyon.

"Whoa!" said Terry.

The rest of us just gawked. The canyon was beginning to open up for us, and we realized we were seeing the legendary badlands. Norris turned onto a smaller road and drove past a sign that read Horseshoe Canyon. He headed towards a lookout.

We piled out of the van like zombies, just staring at the scenery in front of us. We walked up to the edge and looked down into the abyss. Before us was something alien on earth. The canyon was brown and grey and purple and had all sorts of layers in it, and it was filled with sandy hills that looked like giant beehives or something. And each beehive was carved like a sculpture, a sculpture maybe the Big Friendly Giant would have made. There were deep lines and waves and curves in them. Far off in the canyon you could see patches of green grass, pathways, and caves, places you just knew you had to explore. Some of the hills looked as though they had faces, monster faces, and at their bottoms there seemed to be giant dinosaur feet. The parental units have some paintings by this guy named Salvador Dalí. He painted stuff that looks like it comes out of your dreams. This canyon, here in what we had thought was a boring stretch of Canada, seemed as though it had been put together by Salvador Dalí, except it was even weirder. I remembered standing right at the edge of Niagara Falls and having this sensation that I'd like to just jump in. It felt the same way here. I wanted to dive into this wide-open canyon in the badlands of Alberta.

"When the Blackfoot Nation ruled here, long ago," said Norris, "they believed this place was haunted."

That made perfect sense. Haunted. But still, I wanted to climb down in there and walk around until I dropped, edge down some of these sheer cliffs into dreamland. And I knew the other guys did, too. I could tell by the looks on their faces. The sun was beginning to set, and there was a sort of orange glow over everything.

"We have to go," said Ophelia. "We're due at the museum in less than an hour."

"Can we go down in there for a minute?" asked the Bomb.

"Down in there?!" snapped Ophelia.

"Uh, not now," replied Norris. "We may do some camping later on, somewhere in the badlands. Not here. We have to get going."

Back in the van, on the move again, we were all quiet, but I noticed that a couple of the guys were kind of rocking back and forth a little, like the way you get before a big game.

Soon the land flattened out and got boring again. Then we approached the outskirts of Drumheller.

Now, I've been to a few places in this country— the parental units are always travelling around and they've taken me with them a few times. I've been to Newfoundland, for example, and even spent some time in a little ghost-town island off the coast. I've been up to the snowy north of Ontario, and I've checked out just about everything Toronto has to offer. But I've never seen anything like Drumheller. It is just a little town, about eight thousand folks, and they are folks, just down-home types, pretty easygoing. However, they all live in the Land of Oz.

The first thing I noticed was that we were descending, going down on a suddenly twisting road with hills rising all around us. Big bad badlands. Then everything opened up and we realized that we were actually in one of those huge canyons, like the one at

Horseshoe. We saw the sign for Drumheller with a dinosaur on it, a T. rex, and then gas stations, hotels, and that sort of thing—all sitting on land from outer space. Those beehives were all around us, towering over the van, looking even more spectacular because we were among them. We rolled on past their feet, their big dinosaur feet. We had been told that quite a few science fiction movies had been filmed around here. Perfect.

Norris turned on the radio. Country music came blaring out, music we normally would have groaned about. But somehow it sounded different as we stared out at the badlands. It was a fitting soundtrack. There were no words, no twang or complaining voice, just the sound of guitars and fiddles playing fast over a thumping bass. It sounded like the devil's music to me as we went down, down into "Drum."

It faded out and a deep voice, like a salesman's, filled the van.

"Welcome to Drumheller. You are listening to tourism radio for our beautiful region, and you are now in the land of the dinosaurs. Seventy-five million years ago, just outside your windows, creatures as big as houses thundered about on this land, huge, reptile-like beings who engaged in desperate battles to survive, not only against the elements, but also against the sharp teeth, powerful jaws, and rapacious appetites of one another. Drumheller: where history becomes reality, where giants once roamed the earth. In a moment, we'll begin our tour."

The devil music began again.

"Can we, uh, listen to something else?" I asked. "Just until that music stops."

Norris turned the dial.

"This is CBC Calgary," said a smooth voice. "One of the nation's most vicious criminals is still on the loose in southern Alberta."

I noticed Norris glancing at Ophelia.

"The Reptile," continued the announcer. "Seven feet tall, capable of murder at any moment, able to withstand almost any hardship. He was once described by a prison guard as a human being who preys on others. Reports indicate that he might be headed northeast towards the badlands. In fact, he might already—"

Snap.

Norris turned off the radio. Just cracked it off.

"Why did you shut it down, sir?" I asked.

There was no answer at first.

"Who's this Reptile dude?" asked Rhett.

We all looked at each other.

"Not our concern," said Norris. "Not yet, anyway. We are going to the museum, indoors. To sleep with the dinosaurs."

I looked up to the hills of the badlands. They just about touched the big blue sky. I scanned the horizon. There was something about that distant line that gave me an eerie feeling. No matter where I looked, it seemed to be flickering, as if there were something moving around on the edge, as if someone were up there... watching.

2

DINOSAUR HALL

We drove into downtown Drumheller. Once we were there, the place didn't seem so weird. It was just a small town, really, with fast-food joints and some hotels on the outskirts, and then you came into an older area where the banks, churches, and stores and offices were. Even the big grain elevator was something we were getting used to—we'd seen one in just about every town we'd gone through in Alberta. Out there they are as plentiful as hockey rinks. And we saw tons of rinks, too. The kids in the west can play the game, no doubt about it. So everything was pretty normal.

Except for the dinosaurs standing around.

First we spotted a big, gentle sauropod of some sort not far from the *Drumheller Mail* office, then a triceratops hunched over near the Yavis Family Restaurant, and finally a little pack of vicious dromaeosaurs that looked about ready to rip down First Avenue past the post office on a slash-and-kill mission.

"These nearly full-scale models were made by Drumheller residents Tig Seland and Murray Olsen many years ago, boys. Take a close look and see if you can name them," said Norris as he headed towards the bridge that crossed the Red Deer River at the other end of town.

Yawn.

But then he turned his head to the right and almost immediately forgot what he had asked. He had spotted something that nearly made him drive over the railing and into the water. We all noticed it, too.

"Holy sh—," exclaimed Ophelia and then clammed up.

We didn't even laugh. We were too busy gawking. Over to our right, just past a park and in front of a tourism building and the local rink, was the biggest dinosaur on earth. The biggest dinosaur that had ever been on earth! It was green and yellow and very T. rex.

Its mouth was open as if ready to devour, and it was taking a step forward, towards us. It was more than twenty metres high!

"That," said Norris, gulping, "is called the world's biggest dinosaur. It is a central tourist attraction in the downtown Drumheller area."

"Why does he always have to sound like he's reading out of a book?" whispered Bomb, rolling his eyes.

I noticed some stairs leading into the giant dino and some people looking out the mouth.

"We are *climbing* that baby," I said to the guys.

"And hanging Ophelia from its tonsils," cracked Terry.

"Care to share the joke with us, gentlemen?" asked Norris.

"We, uh…" I looked around. "We were just laughing at the big doors on the rink."

In the nick of time, I had seen a big dinosaur head painted on the Zamboni entrance to the arena. You drove in through its open mouth.

Then we passed something else unexpected. It was a movie set. Or it had been. The crew was putting the lights and cameras away, loading them into trucks and big trailers. *Dinosaur Wars II* read a sign, and I could just see part of the company logo on a truck door. "Scare…"

it began—I couldn't read the rest. They had lots of props. One guy was loading things that actually looked like bones into a big container. He kept spilling them. As one truck pulled away, I noticed it had a California license plate. It headed towards the highway that went southeast, out of town.

Another surprise about Drumheller was how green it was downtown. In fact, many of the valleys out there were. The river was beautiful, and there looked to be some pretty nice houses and park areas along its banks. As we drove through, we saw an old school on a side street and a group of about eight kids peeling along on bikes. They cut in front of the van, whipping past just close enough to make Norris touch his brakes. Then we all turned and watched them launch themselves, one after the other, over the sidewalk on the other side of the street.

Standing there were five girls, trying to look totally unimpressed. But for some reason they glanced over when our van went by, as if they could just tell we were from out of town. They looked at us and we looked at them. Their clothes stood out, almost like movie costumes that they had bought at a second-hand store, and they all wore a little makeup. One of them seemed like their leader, a brown-haired girl who was wearing an old-fashioned dress. She locked eyes with me for a second, just a second, but she really seemed to stare. She had a different kind of look.

We drove on past some tourist shops, each one with a sign advertising prehistoric fossils for sale, and headed for the other end of town. We could see the badlands rising up again to the north, but we turned left and moved west along the far side of the river. A sign said we were on the North Dinosaur Trail, and after about thirty seconds, we saw another marker, Royal Tyrrell Museum of Palaeontology. It read, "6 kms."

Tonight, we were going to sleep in this world-famous place. And not in some sort of room made up for kids, or out in the lobby or anything like that. We were going to bunk down right in Dinosaur Hall. Right among the giant lizards themselves. We could hardly wait.

The road wound along the river for a while. There were small museums in old houses and little subdivisions on the green land beside the river. To our right the terrain was growing more desolate again. Hills loomed above. We were in Midland Provincial Park. And to think I'd figured a park had to be green, or maybe have a blade of grass!

Before long Norris slowed the van, turned, and drove along a very smooth, perfectly paved road that twisted its way through several beehive hills. Around another corner we could see a large, clear pond with some fountains in it, and an outdoor patio for a restaurant. Given where we were, in the middle of Mars, I didn't expect to see a very big building. Boy, was I wrong. It came into our view and just kept growing, made of concrete and glass, fairly flat but stretching out across the wasteland. It looked like a modern place set in an ancient land.

As we passed by the front entrance on our way towards the parking lot, we could see two triceratops on one side and a couple of raptors of some sort on the other, up on pedestals, racing along after each other. They looked like more dromaeosaurs with their frightening, three-bladed claws. Then there was a much bigger one, probably an albertosaurus, I wasn't sure. It glared at the others, muscular legs in motion, razor teeth bared, and its eyes, yellow with black pupils, latched on to its prey. They were monster lizards in a little game of deadly catch.

"The albertosaurus, though slightly smaller than the *Tyrannosaurus rex*, was at least as lethal. With its quick, mobile movements and powerful jaws, it was a predator nonpareil," said Norris. Ophelia smiled at him, pleased as punch with his impressive vocabulary.

"Gag me, with a shovel," said Terry under his breath.

We would have been out of the parking lot and into the museum in about two seconds flat, except Norris and Ophelia took about an hour getting their stuff unloaded. We all grabbed our bags—four Metro Toronto Hockey League duffle bags to be exact—pitched them out the back doors onto the pavement, and leapt out after them. Then we waited. Norris took out his suitcase (about the size of Oakville, and the same green colour as our van); his big, brown, fat briefcase that always had papers hanging out of it and looked old enough to have been brought to Canada by Jacques Cartier; a laptop, which he quickly bashed into the side of the van; and finally his big belt with its pouch, which he then proceeded to wrap around his bulging waist. He kept so many things in that briefcase that we couldn't believe it—tons of books and maps and markers and flashlights and who-knows-what-else. One of these days I expected him to reach in and draw out a large-screen television or something. Then he stuck his head into the glove compartment (it looked like his whole head went in) and got out his pocket-protector and about twenty-seven pens and stuck them into the little pocket of the white shirt he was wearing. He always wore white shirts.

But that was nothing compared to Ophelia. She had six suitcases. Six. Count 'em. And Norris unloaded them all. Then she took out some sort of leather carrying bag that was the shape of a hat and then a heavy little case that looked like it might hold a semi-automatic pistol or something.

By the time Norris had all her stuff out (and he insisted that she allow him to unload it all himself), we already had our earbuds in, grooving to some tunes, and we were booting the hackeysack around the lot to each other. I noticed that heavy little gun-case out of the corner of my eye. No way I was carrying that.

"Dylan Maples," said Ophelia, in that high-pitched whine of hers, "you shall carry my makeup bag."

She handed me the gun-case. Oh man!

Norris soon had the other guys loaded up with luggage and we edged across the lot towards the museum. How embarrassing!

Suddenly, Norris stopped and set down the four bags he was carrying (Ophelia just had her purse, though it looked like it weighed about a tonne). He felt around in the pockets of his shirt and pants.

"Dear," he said. "Dear, I think I've forgotten my glasses."

There was dead silence. Norris looked at us...
through his thick, horn-rimmed glasses.

"Uh, dearest...you are...uh...wearing them," said
Ophelia, looking at the ground.

Norris clutched at his face. "And so I am...never
mind. Proceed."

We headed for the museum entrance, all of us
holding back laughter like you'd be holding back pee
if you hadn't gone to the washroom for about a week.

It was kind of dark in the hallway entrance, but then
it opened up into an area with a gift shop on one side
and information and ticket booths on the other. Norris
and Ophelia marched us right over to the booths and
announced who we were. Then we sat down near the
gift shop and waited for our host.

As we loafed around, taking turns punching each
other on the shoulder, four kids came through the
doors. Two of them were girls. I recognized the one
who had looked right at me in Drumheller. She still had
that dress on, a sort of movie-star one from an antique
shop...though I mean that in a good way...kind of. She
looked at me again. Then they started moving towards
us. *Hello.* A man dressed as badly as Norris came
through the doors just behind them and walked over
to the booths.

"Hey," said Rhett, "check out the hayseeds at twelve o'clock."

They stopped before they reached us and stood around, most of them looking a little awkward. But every now and then that girl would kind of glance at me. She didn't seem awkward at all.

That was when I noticed that Norris and Ophelia were talking to the man who had come in with these kids. Moments later they were all walking in our direction, motioning the eight of us to come closer together.

"Hello, boys, my name is Mr. Tinman and I am principal of Emerald Public School here in the great Dinosaur Valley town of Drumheller."

Another speechmaker.

"We welcome you to our town and hope you have a wonderful stay with us. These four young people are students at our school, and they will be your hosts for tonight. Please introduce yourselves."

For a moment no one said anything. We all kind of looked at the floor. Then the girl spoke up, loudly and confidently. "I'm Dorothy. Dorothy Osborne," she said.

"Dylan Maples," I replied firmly, and stepped forward. For some reason I took her hand and shook it. It was soft and warm. She smiled.

"Oh, how cute," said Bomb under his breath. I glared at him.

The other kids then announced their names as if they were robots. One of them was some guy named Stockwell, a bit of a pinhead we thought. Another was a dude named Ralph in an Oilers sweater, who seemed a bit more reasonable, and then there was a girl named Hanna who was pretty shy and dressed in what I think she thought were pretty cool clothes, her belly button showing beneath a rather tight shirt that could have fit a ten-year-old. None of the rest shook hands, which made me feel like an even bigger idiot. But when I glanced over at Dorothy, it seemed like she couldn't care less.

Then she did something that kind of shocked us all. As we walked towards the main entrance to the exhibits, she got out a couple of pink elastics and put two big pigtails into her reddish-brown hair. I'd never seen a girl with pigtails before, at least one past the age of five. But her friends didn't even seem to notice—no one smirked. Everything that Dorothy did seemed just fine with them.

Then Bomb sort of snickered.

"Problem?" asked Dorothy, looking him right in the eyes.

"Uh…"

"I didn't think so," she said, and she slapped him just above the butt, the way we crank each other in the back of the pants with our sticks after we score a goal. Bomb looked a little startled. I'd never seen that particular expression on his face before.

The museum is set up to kind of explain life right from the very beginning of time. You wind your way around from room to room, moving from very ancient times to the dinosaurs, which are the main thing in the exhibits, and then you finish off with mastodons and cavemen and that sort of stuff.

First up was a big revolving globe in a nearly pitch-black space. It was pretty cool because it almost seemed to be floating there, and the man's voice, describing the creation of the world and life and all that stuff, was kind of deep and spooky. We watched from some carpeted benches nearby, set up like seats in a theatre.

Just as we were leaving that room, the museum official who was going to accompany us, both inside the building and out in the field, arrived. He was a work of art—he actually looked like a dinosaur! A hadrosaur, to be exact: one of those duck-billed, plant-eater types with the forehead that sticks out. Paleontologists had found quite a few of them nearby, and this guy had probably studied them. Studied too many and started looking like them! He was fairly tall with very long arms that hung down at his sides, and he walked slightly stooped, with rounded shoulders. His lips stuck out a little, and a pile of thick hair swooped way out over his forehead.

Without even saying hello, he started talking to us.

"I love dinosaurs," he announced.

"That's because you are one," said Terry into my ear.

All the other Alberta kids were paying attention, but Dorothy looked over at me, and I could see she knew exactly what Terry and I were thinking. Her eyes were smiling. I tried not to laugh. She was working at it, too.

Hadrosaur-man was actually a pretty nice guy. Lyons was his real name. And he did indeed love dinosaurs. In fact, sometimes he seemed more like a kid than any of us. He would get all excited when he showed us a specimen, and then his eyes would get watery and his voice would rise. In fact, that happened with the very first thing he showed us. It was an albertosaurus—a real, live, fossilized skeleton of one, right in front of our eyes, more than 65 million years old. It was nearly ten metres long!

"Evil!" said Terry excitedly under his breath.

"This dinosaur was found just a few years ago about a kilometre from the front door of the museum. It is one of the most complete prehistoric skeletons in existence, though what we are looking at is not actual bone but a fossil, or bone essentially turned to stone. Mr. Albertosaurus here was found in the typical position of a dead dinosaur: in a 'death pose.' The tendons in his neck, and in his tail, contracted after he expired, pulling his head upward towards his body, just as his tail swirled in a similar fashion."

It almost looked to be in agony, its head pulled back and its mouth open. Wow.

"Can you imagine a lizard that size just walking around out here?" whispered Dorothy into my ear.

"Uh, yeah."

"You can?" she said. "I'm still working on that. Remember, if he saw you, he'd eat you alive. And I mean alive. He'd hunt you down, Dylan Maples."

As she moved off with the others, I just stood there. I could imagine it all right. I imagined things far too easily. It was kind of embarrassing. An image of the albertosaurus coming right at me flashed through my mind. I closed my eyes. *Stop it.*

The others were headed up a ramp, and I hurried to catch up.

"Cool. Cool," I heard Rhett say. And that's saying something for him, because he's pretty cool himself, not one to get too excited or show much emotion. He's a defenceman, big and strong—one might even say a little fat, though that one wouldn't be me. And nothing ever rattles him, even under pressure.

As we neared the top of the ramp we could see these massive skeletons looming above us. Hadrosaur-man soon brought us right beneath them. They were giants, two storeys high. Their heads were the size of our entire bodies, their teeth like butcher knives, and they seemed as long as whales. But they were all lizard. Our host was beaming, his face almost red with excitement.

"Ladies and gentlemen...T. rex!" was all he said.

"What's the other one?" asked Terry. A T. rex and another giant dinosaur were facing off against each other, almost snarling, it seemed. The enemy looked just as big, maybe even bigger.

"That, my young friend, is a giganotosaurus, discovered in the wilds of Argentina. Paleontologists now believe that it is the largest meat-eating dinosaur ever found. It weighed anywhere from six to eight tonnes."

"Bigger than T. rex?" I asked.

"By a talon or two," he said, "though a talon on a T. rex was more than half a metre long."

"So," said Bomb, "who would win if they got it on?"

I could see Norris cringing.

"Got it on?"

"He means if they fought," clarified Dorothy.

"Oh," replied our host. "Well, uh, they probably wouldn't fight. They don't seem to have been from the same region or time period, and they were both meat-eaters anyway, not interested in each other as prey. These hunters, theropods as we call them—that means 'beast foot'—tended to look for more vulnerable meals: plant-eaters, often smallish ones, sickly ones, the way a lion might search for the easiest gazelle to grab from a herd. Maybe one that had strayed."

"Even still," said Bomb, "who'd win? Who'd be the killer here?"

There was silence for a moment. Norris looked as though he'd like to say something, but he didn't.

"Well, even though giganotosaurus was a little larger, he didn't quite have the powerful jaws or the speed of T—"

"I thought so," said Bomb.

"Shall we move on?" snapped Norris. He pulled Bomb to the back of the pack as we walked towards the next exhibit.

Some of the facts on the walls about these freaky lizards were unbelievable. There was a plant-eater called the argentinosaurus that apparently weighed more than a hundred tonnes. That was pretty amazing in itself, but what really blew me away was that the giganotosaurus used to *hunt* it! Giganto was described as a meat-slicer and T. rex, a bone-crusher. Neither one did much chewing. They just ripped open their prey and swallowed big chunks whole. We all thought that was pretty cool.

Our tour continued. We saw scientists working on fossilized bones behind glass, all kinds of models of every dinosaur from every era, and a real display of plants from dinosaur days. We read information about great fossil discoveries (a stone dinosaur egg was on display, found in the area by a kid our age), how fossils were preserved, how the badlands came to exist, and what the land was like in ancient days. There were dinosaurs flying through the air, and even prehistoric creatures in water. Our host took us behind the scenes and showed us "Dinosaur Alley," where they kept some awesome remains. He told us how scientists used air-powered tools to dig them out, and that they had to lift them up in burlap bags and hoist them away with helicopters. Least interesting were the lectures about how dinosaurs were classified (the lizard-hipped and the bird-hipped, and, of course, carnivores and vegetarians). And the facts that were spewed at us about

the three time periods—Triassic, Jurassic, Cretaceous—
of the dinosaurs' Mesozoic Era, 250 to 65 million years
ago, weren't too thrilling, either.

What *we* liked were the gory, big-screen movies and
the interactive stuff. The video games were excellent
too. Me and the guys jumped onto some of them and
had a ball. Rhett was as cool as ever, Bomb was pretty
impatient, and Terry, of course, brain that he is, could
navigate through everything he found without even
following the instructions. The scenes where we got to
be meat-eating hunters chasing down and killing plant-
eaters were the best. It was just so gruesome! Dorothy
liked it as much as us, but in a different way. She didn't
get quite as excited. I hate to say she was mature about
it...but she was. And every time she played, she sure
played to win.

It was sort of a whirlwind tour, and Hadrosaur-man
promised us we would have more time later to look at
everything much closer. But first they wanted us in the
cafeteria to eat, and then we were to get to bed. We'd
had a long day.

By the time we got back from dinner, the museum
had closed, and we were the only ones in the building.
Norris and Ophelia kind of lagged behind on purpose,
and began a conversation they thought none of us could

hear. But sound carried better when the building was quiet, so we heard quite a bit of what they were saying. The words "the Reptile" kept coming up, and Ophelia seemed scared. "But what if…?" she said once or twice, each time her voice trailing off. Norris tried to calm her with his answers. She didn't seem to be buying them.

Up ahead, me and the guys were walking together, trying to listen to every word. I guess we'd all started to get pretty serious expressions on our faces. But when we noticed each other's grim looks, we tried to pretend that we didn't care. Rhett smirked first, then the rest of us. Ophelia was *so* paranoid.

We walked across the hallway entrance, past the albertosaurus-death-pose skeleton, and other displays, and then into Dinosaur Hall, the museum's coolest room. In it were lifelike models of the giant reptiles, so real that they seemed almost alive again. They stood in sand and among trees, and behind them the walls were painted to look like the landscape they had once lived in.

We were actually going to sleep here. The girls would be on one side of the big Cretaceous-era display with Ophelia, and the boys on the other, with Norris, a good ten metres apart. I bedded down in my sleeping bag underneath a T. rex and looked up at its face. This was going to be awesome.

3

A DARK DREAM

"**D**ylan?"

It was Bomb. In the darkness.

"Yeah."

"You awake?"

"No. I'm fast asleep."

"I'm sleeping too, Bomber," said Terry, "but I have the amazing ability to talk to you while I do it."

"Very funny. But if you're all asleep, who's snoring?"

"Newcombe," said the rest of us, together.

Then there was another sound.

"Hi."

We all froze. It was a girl's voice.

"I'm sleeping too," said Dorothy.

"Are you, uh, out of bed?" I asked.

"Brought it with me," she said. "You guys have a better spot here. They have us down with a bunch of little plant-eaters. And by that I don't mean Stockwell and his buddies."

"I heard that!" said a low voice, rather angry, just as we all started laughing. It was the Stock-man himself. "Go to sleep!" he whined.

"If you ignore him, he usually goes away," whispered Dorothy, leaning very close to me.

"What about the others?"

"Hanna's cool, and you couldn't wake up Ralph with a power tool."

"We could try," I said.

"Man," sighed Dorothy, looking up at the T. rex, "you guys get *all* the meat-eaters. At least they could have given us a lambeosaurus—imagine, eight tonnes of veggie dino. Or even a quetzalcoatlus swooping around above us with that twelve-metre wingspan. That would have been neat."

"What's Ophelia's condition?" I asked.

"Just listen."

We all stopped talking. In the distance, beyond the sound of Norris's deep wheezing, we could hear a slightly higher-pitched snore. We all laughed, and then stopped, afraid we were being too loud. The echo of our laughter faded down Dinosaur Hall.

"So," said Dorothy, "what do they have lined up for you guys over the next few days?"

"Stuff," said Rhett dryly. He wasn't pleased that she was in our territory.

"Oh, that's brilliant," snapped Dorothy. "What *kind* of stuff, genius?"

Back home nobody talked like that to Rhett. He was even quieter than usual for the next little while.

"I believe," this was Terry's voice, "we will be excavating dinosaur bones around here, then assisting with transforming actual fossils into models in the museum, and it has been said we may travel over to Dinosaur Provincial Park and tour the restricted area."

"Are you always like that?" asked Dorothy.

"Like what?"

"Such a brain. Why didn't you just say you were going on a bone dig and down to the park?"

"Why don't you shut your mouth, pigtails?"

That was Bomb. He wasn't one to take a lot of guff from girls.

"Is that you, blondie?" said Dorothy. "The one with the funny clothes?"

Bomb has blond hair and is an excellent winger. He's not always the deepest thinker, but he's a funny guy and he loves to goof around. He wears some pretty neat stuff too…I think. But regardless of what I thought about either of them, I had to jump into this conversation.

"Can we call a truce here?" I asked.

"Absolutely," said Dorothy, without hesitation. "Sorry, guys. Just being myself."

This was one unpredictable girl. She wasn't very big, and she looked kind of sweet and innocent, with a girlish voice. Most of the time she didn't seem like a tomboy, but man, could she trade punches when she was talking with us. Then suddenly she'd be just as nice as the way she looked. Not that I was paying a lot of attention to the way she looked.

"Uh, sure," said the Bomb, a little surprised.

"Sure," said Terry.

Rhett was still quiet.

"From what I hear, we might not get to do all the things we had planned," I said.

"Really?" asked Dorothy. "Why?" She sounded disappointed.

"The Reptile," said Rhett.

"That weirdo? What does he have to do with you guys?"

"We don't know for sure," I said, "but we've been noticing how much Newcombe and the wife have been talking about him, always whispering, too. We're supposed to be here for twelve days and spend a lot of it out in the park."

"Yeah," added Terry, "but we're getting worried Newcombe is going to cancel some of the trip, maybe take us home earlier."

"They seem pretty freaked out by this Reptile guy," said Bomb.

"I don't blame them," replied Dorothy.

"You don't?"

"My father says he's the worst criminal we've ever had in Alberta. They say he killed a kid about our age. They found the kid's bones somewhere—in a cave, I think. But my dad says they think he's killed even more people."

"Kids?" asked Rhett. I was surprised at the tone of his voice. He didn't sound like the steady defenceman we all knew.

"I wouldn't be surprised."

"But do you really think he'd come here?"

"Why not? The badlands are perfect. You can just disappear into them. And finding someone out there—especially someone like this guy, who they say could live on air if he had to—that's going to be nearly impossible. I bet he's here right now."

There was silence for a moment. I looked up and saw the T. rex snarling down at me.

"When you say 'here,'" I asked, "what do you mean?"

"She means right in this building," said Terry in a weird voice, "creeping down Dinosaur Hall, looking for your sleeping bag, Maples!"

"Shut up, Singh!"

"Boo!" said Bomb.

We heard a noise near us. We all went silent.

"Yes, dear, I have clean underwear on, yes, in case of an accident…yes…yes…yes…."

It was Newcombe, talking in his sleep. We couldn't hold back our laughter and we all buried our heads in our sleeping bags, just letting loose.

"What I meant was," said Dorothy, still giggling, "I think he's probably here, in the Drumheller area, in Dinosaur Valley."

We all stopped laughing.

"Are you serious?" asked Terry.

"Deadly. When you look at when he left Calgary and the direction he was going…I think he's here."

There was silence in Dinosaur Hall.

We didn't talk much after that. After a while Dorothy said good night and we heard her shuffling along the floor in her sleeping bag, back towards the girls' area. Then my eyelids started getting heavy. The last thing I saw was the vague outline of that T. rex head and its huge teeth, sharp as razors.

I drifted into another world. It was seventy-five million years ago. It was hot, even muggier than it gets on an August day in Toronto when the pollution index is high. I was alone, and sweating, despite being half-naked and standing still. The land was sandy, muddy in places; there were ponds and swamps filled with lily pads and thick green vegetation. Huge ferns towered over me, and so did spooky cypress trees with moss hanging from them like vampires' capes. The moon looked twice the size it should have. And yet, something told me I hadn't gone far. I was still in Canada, in Alberta. In the distance I could hear growls and shrieks, inhuman sounds. But they weren't like the cry of any animal I had ever heard. These creatures sounded very large. Like giants.

Then there was another sound, quiet and distant at first but soon growing louder and coming nearer. A rhythmic, thudding sound. Footsteps! The ground shook more with each pounding step. I scurried over to a tree and flattened myself against the trunk. Now every step was like an earthquake. And before long, a beast, unlike any I had ever seen and bigger than I ever could have imagined, emerged out of the trees. *A dinosaur! A* lambeosaurus, fifteen metres long! It looked like a barn, except it was moving, and breathing, and it was very frightened. It turned its head and glanced around. Then it stood perfectly still. I could see that one of its feet was lame, and it looked old. As it stood there, listening, silence slowly descended on the jungle, as if every other animal that had been growling, shrieking, and trumpeting knew that it was time to listen for dear life. I stared way up at the dinosaur's huge face.

Suddenly there was thunder in the trees near us. In a flash a giant lizard leapt forward, seized the lambeosaurus, and slammed it down. The thud shook the ground as if the whole earth were moving. Cowering against the tree, I could see the massive head of a living, breathing *Tyrannosaurus rex*, fluorescent green and yellow, its jaws wide, its knife-like teeth penetrating the lambeosaurus's long neck, its claws slicing into thick hide. It roared like fifty lions at a kill, the noise vibrating against my skin and making the hair stand up on the back of my neck. It tore open its huge prey, slashing the skin. Blood spurted out in a great gush, and I could hear the giant bones crunching.

I couldn't watch so I turned and ran. Then, for some reason, *the T. rex was after me!* It shot through the trees on its massive legs. I was a mole it was going to swipe up and devour. As I ran I began to see other creatures, tiny mammals, scurrying underground. I remembered seeing these mouse-like animals on display at the museum. "These cowering, frightened little beasts," Mr. Lyons, the Hadrosaur-man, had said, "are our ancestors." I wasn't doing much better than they were now.

Sprinting and stumbling forward, I saw other dinosaurs looking at me: a big, spectacularly coloured corythosaurus, calm and camouflaged, using its skills to survive; the armour-plated triceratops turning its horn to meet its foe; quetzalcoatlus swooping down to see the chase; and troodons, birdlike and not much bigger than me, knifing by at top speed, shrieking, wondering if they should rip me open with their deadly claws and eat parts of me as we ran, stealing a meal from the king himself. But before long, to my surprise, I seemed to be getting away. And slowly everything became quiet again. Somehow, I had escaped.

I stood alone in the trees, my chest heaving. I listened to my heavy breaths. Soon they began to lessen. I sat, still listening intently. The silence continued. I lay down and looked up at the blue sky above the strange-looking trees.

Then something emerged in that blue…a massive head, yellow eyes on fire. *The T. rex was above me!* Its teeth were fully bared; drool dripped from its mouth. The face seemed almost human, the head shaved clean. Its jaws snapped wide open and it lowered its head to rip me open.

I woke up.

High above in the darkness, the head of the museum's T. rex was glaring at me, and I screamed.

Boy, would I ever regret that.

Slowly kids started waking up: "Eh?" "What's up?" "Who screamed?" "Was that you, Maples?" "What a wimp." "Should I get Mommy on the phone?"

Did they ever give it to me. Even that pinhead Stockwell laid a snide comment on me. But Dorothy was quiet; she never said a word. Over the next few days, while my buds wouldn't let my blood-curdling, late-night scream die, Dorothy would never even let on that she'd woken up. But I saw her, sitting up in the darkness of Dinosaur Hall, in a spot between the boys' and girls' areas, looking at me, just staring, as if she were thinking. There really was something different about that girl.

"Mr. Maples, are you all right?"

It was Ophelia. As far as I could tell, Newcombe hadn't budged. In fact, in the second of silence that followed her question, I heard the full blast of another snore. Dead to the world.

"Yes, Mrs. Newcombe, I'm fine."

"Nightmare?"

"Uh…yes."

"Nothing to be ashamed of. Even my Norris has a dark dream or two."

"Not a big bad brute like him…" mumbled Bomber inside his sleeping bag.

"Do you have a question, Mr. Connors?" asked Ophelia.

"No, ma'am. But do you think Mr. Maples would like me to hold his hand?"

"That will be quite enough, Mr. Connors. Everyone terminate conversation. And back to sleep. Thank you." With that she turned and disappeared into the darkness.

Other than a discussion among the buds about whether or not I'd peed the bed—one that they conducted as if they were investigating some sort of serious issue they'd just seen on the national news—there wasn't much more said about it. I think the guys were too tired to really lay into me. They were saving it for morning.

As I settled back in and stared up at that T. rex head again, something dawned on me. The huge meat-eater in my dream had indeed had a human face. And I had seen it somewhere. I racked my brain. Then it came to me. I had seen that face at the airport on the front page of the *Calgary Herald*. The dinosaur that had nearly eaten me was none other than "the Reptile" himself.

OUTSIDE IN THE DARKNESS, *a tall man dressed in black was stealthily making his way down out of the badlands hills, glancing around, listening. The museum sat beneath him, like a toy. But his dark eyes were focused on a distant thought. He was planning something. He held a bone in his hand. He looked at it, and smiled.*

Suddenly, a light came on in the building, a dim one, glowing in Dinosaur Hall. The tall man noticed. His head turned as if he were sensing prey.

Minutes later he had reached lower ground, then he approached the fountains, and then the museum entrance. He ran his hands along the three-bladed claw of one of the dromaeosaurs on its pedestal outside.

That light intrigued him. He climbed a wall like a spider and peered down through a skylight into the Hall. Children!

They were sitting up in their sleeping bags, speaking to a female teacher. One of them looked a little frightened.

A few minutes later he was back out in the badlands, that bone still in his hand. Soon he came to an open pit, filled with the fossilized bones of dinosaurs. He flung his bone high into the air, not looking at where it landed. The tall man smiled again. Then he turned and fled into the hills, his black clothing glistening in the moonlight.

4

BONES

The first thing I saw the next morning was Newcombe in a housecoat, carrying his toothbrush. What a sight. Soon he was barking at us and we were all "up and at 'em," as he put it.

Even when we were dressed and ready to roll, we all sort of looked as if we had been sleeping in garbage cans or something. I hate combing my hair, mostly because even when I do comb it, it still looks like a mess. A "riot of black hair" my mom calls it. Dad says it always looks like someone cut it with a lawnmower. Actually, no one wants their hair to really look combed, so I wasn't so badly off. I even heard one of the girls back at school whisper to her friend that she thought it looked kind of cool. I never told anyone about that, no one. But afterwards, I *really* didn't want to comb it any more.

So we were all looking kind of grungy, even for us. We were rubbing our eyes and stumbling out of Dinosaur Hall, moving down towards the cafeteria. That was when I realized that Dorothy Osborne was with us. She had just sort of materialized, like some sort of alien from *Star Trek*—not a gross one, though. And *she* didn't look like she'd been sleeping in a garbage can. She looked all neat and tidy, everything in place. Girls have this weird ability to do that. Her hair wasn't in pigtails now; it was all combed out. And I mean *combed*, like it was glowing or something.

"What's on the schedule today?"

"Stuff," I said.

She laughed.

"I think maybe we're going on the dig."

"One of the museum's 'Day Digs'? Really? They're pretty awesome."

"But you know what I really want to do?"

"What?"

"I want to go hiking in the badlands. That's just *got* to be cool."

"It is. We do it all the time. Done it since we were little. Kids get lost in the badlands sometimes, you know."

"Really?"

"Yeah. And there are scorpions and coyotes and black widow spiders and rattlesnakes and all sorts of stuff around. And weirdos live out there too, in caves. Or at least that's what people say. I've never seen any of them."

"Caves?"

"Well, the story is that when the area first got settled by white people, some of the men who came here to mine the coal didn't have enough money for houses, so they just put roofs into the earth above the caves in the badlands cliffs and lived there."

"Cool."

"And some of them, or their ghosts or something, are still there."

"Do you believe in ghosts?" I asked her quietly, hoping she wouldn't think that was a totally moronic question.

But Dorothy Osborne was full of surprises. She didn't even blink. "Sure," she said. "Saw one once."

"So did I," I sort of whispered.

"You did?" She didn't whisper, and she actually looked intrigued. "Where?"

"In Newfoundland," I said, a little louder. "In a place called Ireland's Eye, an abandoned island almost out in the ocean. It was awesome. I'll never forget it."

"The one I saw was in the badlands."

"Wow."

"Late one night, a friend and I were out there, and we saw something. It didn't seem human, because it was actually very small…but it looked like it was standing up on two legs…it had these yellow eyes…" She paused, as if seeing the ghost again. "We were a long piece away," she added quickly. "So maybe we were kind of imagining it. We were never sure what it was."

"Weren't you afraid to go out there after that?"

"No. Well…maybe a bit at night. But there's nothing wrong with being a little afraid. Kind of gets the adrenaline going. Besides, Drumheller is so far away from everything, it's nice to have *some* excitement, even if it scares you. But I wouldn't want to get lost out there this week." Before I could say anything else, the teachers called us all to attention in the cafeteria. Soon we were settled in to demolish about a million pancakes and sausages. Newcombe sat in a corner with the adults and read the day's *Calgary Herald*. He didn't seem too interested in his meal. After a while he lowered his head and had a long conversation with Ophelia. Then he got up and went over to a pay phone. It seemed like he stayed there for about half an hour, talking, with a very serious look on his face.

By the time he'd returned to Ophelia, conferred with her again, and headed over to us, we were all done. We'd lined up two tables and, using crumpled-up newspaper for pucks, were playing our own version of table-top hockey—hit the goalie in the face and it's in. Ralph turned out to be at least as good as any of us, Hanna surprised Terry and nailed him right in the bugle with a slapshot, and Dorothy, of course, was right into it, big time. That Stockwell guy wouldn't even play, said we were too noisy or something.

We started straightening up as the Newcombes and Mr. Tinman clomped over. The Bomb was facing their way and gave us a signal. They looked as if someone had just stolen their Christmas presents.

"Boys, we may have to operate on an abbreviated schedule," said Newcombe.

"Which means?" asked Bomber.

"Which means we might not stay here for the whole eight days," said Ophelia. She looked kind of relieved, actually.

"Why?" asked Rhett.

"Never mind *why* for now," continued Norris. "I will tell you later. What matters is that we have some very fine things to do here in the Dinosaur Valley of Drumheller, nestled amongst the badlands of Alberta, and we can manage to do quite a number of them in the four or five days we will have available to us."

"Four or five days?" I said. Bomber and Terry groaned.

"That's right. Now we—"

"It's the Reptile, isn't it?" said Terry matter-of-factly.

Newcombe paused. He looked at Ophelia and then at Tinman, and then continued as though Terry hadn't spoken.

"Today is our day to dig up some real dinosaur fossils. That's what our minds will be trained on, nothing else. Right, Mr. Tinman?"

"Yes, of course, Mr. Newcombe. And the mind of one of our own pupils will be trained upon it as well." He turned to his students. "Let's see if we can provide some good old-fashioned Drumheller hospitality by supplying these out-of-towners with a knowledgeable companion on their exciting excavating adventure. I need a volunteer. Hands?"

I glanced at Dorothy. Her hand shot up. Unfortunately, so did Stockwell's. *If we have to put up with that pinhead all day,* I thought, *I'll throw up.*

"Um." Mr. Tinman looked back and forth between his two students. "I think it would be nice to have a lady on the tour. Dorothy Osborne, you may go on the dig. And you will have the option of accompanying our guests for the next three days as well. That is, if you feel up to being their hostess?"

"I do," said Dorothy.

She had this funny look on her face. It was sort of a smile. But there was more to it than that. It was sly. What was she thinking about? Making us feel at home? Or how she might scare the life out of us city boys?

ABOUT HALF AN HOUR LATER we were heading out from the museum on a hike, right into the badlands. We weren't too pleased about the possibility of our trip being shortened, but four or five days seemed a long time away right now—maybe things would change. And besides, this dig promised to be fun. Mr. Lyons, the Hadrosaur-man, was with us, of course, as a guide, and so was Mr. Tinman.

We stopped just a few kilometres away, at a place called Kneehill Creek. This was where Joseph Burr Tyrrell, while doing fieldwork for the Geological Survey of Canada in 1884, had stumbled upon the first dinosaur skull found and documented in the area.

Tyrrell would accomplish many more great things in his career, but it was that one extraordinary moment that put his name on the landmark museum we had slept in the night before.

I could almost imagine him: a young, bearded man with little, wire-rimmed glasses, travelling by canoe down the Red River in the heat of an Alberta summer, mapping the area and examining coal and mineral deposits in the green valleys and up and down the steep cliffs. He would have been used to seeing Blood and Peigan people, and a few scattered white settlers. But then he comes upon another sort of beast entirely, a beast no one has ever heard of, or even imagined. "It is a creature," he will write, "from a time beyond our fathoming."

It's summer. The sun is high; the heat is intense. About to seek shade for lunch, he sees something staring out at him from the side of a hill. It's a skull, nearly as long as a fully-grown man, the fossilized head of a massive, ancient lizard. A few teeth remain: the knife-sized, ripping instruments of a mean, meat-eating predator.

Later investigations would reveal that this dinosaur weighed about two tonnes, was nearly ten metres long, and moved on powerful hind legs that allowed it to run at speeds of up to thirty kilometres an hour. It could tear its victims' limbs apart or crush them in its powerful jaws; it could kick them with massive sledgehammer blows from its giant, muscular legs. This smaller but quicker version of its cousin, the *Tyrannosaurus rex*, was Alberta's very own ancient killing machine. So they called it albertosaurus: "the lizard from Alberta."

These weren't the first dinosaur remains ever discovered, or even the first in Canada, but Tyrrell's find set off a frenzy of searches soon known as the Great Canadian Dinosaur Hunt, and the world's paleontologists began heading for Drumheller and southeastern Alberta.

My mind was far away, imagining those early discoveries of prehistoric life, when I suddenly realized that Hadrosaur-man was telling us something.

The word "dinosaur," he was saying, comes from two Greek words: *deinos*, meaning terrible, and *sauros*, meaning lizard. That was perfect. They were like monsters from some sort of IMAX movie, like salamanders on steroids that were fifty times your size and could rip you in two. Terrible lizards for sure!

Paleontologists, he explained, had made many more amazing discoveries in western Canada: other examples of albertosaurus; three-horned, five-tonne triceratops; herds of huge, plant-eating, duck-billed hadrosaurs;

ankylosaurs with armour-plated eyelids and weapon-tails that ended in big war clubs; and of course a T. rex, the "tyrant" of its day.

Among the adventurers was Charles Sternberg, who came from the United States but stayed in Canada once he discovered the dinosaur treasures of Alberta. Sternberg became one of the country's leading experts on prehistoric life. Another was American Barnum Brown, named for the famous circus impresario and just as bold, who found his way to the bone beds of both Drumheller and what would one day be Dinosaur Provincial Park via the Red Deer River on a ten-metre-long flatboat, complete with tent. He found literally tonnes of incredible, exotic remains.

Hadrosaur-man was leading us right towards some bone beds that were still being dug. But it wasn't as if we were just going to start hacking away in a particularly important one. Skeletal fossils can be pretty fragile. We were going to a pre-arranged site, and there wasn't much chance we were going to stumble upon some sort of amazing discovery on the way there.

The badlands were originally under a huge ancient sea, where all sorts of soft sands and silt had gathered. Then, when the glaciers came and went about fifteen thousand years ago, they just carved up all that soft land. And wind and other natural forces caused even more erosion. That's why they look so freaky, and why they're perfect for dinosaur bones. You can look at the badlands and see many millions of years, levels of our history right in the earth, older as you go lower. The badlands look almost decorated with horizontal stripes of time, each band a slightly different colour. And, once you get 65 million years down, the fossilized bones of those "terrible" giant beasts can be found, exposed by erosion, either in bits and pieces or sometimes in amazing whole stone skeletons, caught in their swirling death poses, lying in their bone beds.

Hadrosaur-man put on a good show of letting us look for some new discovery. We trudged around in what was now burning heat. It was like being out in our very own Canadian desert. We all had hats on and about ten layers of sunscreen. We kind of goofed around a little, aware that we probably wouldn't find anything there. Then, finally, Hadrosaur-man led us to the actual dig site.

We walked for about another kilometre before we came to it, but the effort was worth it. There were a couple of paleontologists already working when we arrived. They stood up, shook hands with us, and began explaining what they were doing.

Before us we could see the partial skeletons of about four dinosaurs, embedded in the dirt. When they'd first started working on this site they'd used larger instruments, but now, as the stone-bones emerged clearly, they were down to using more delicate tools: chisels and little spades, that sort of thing. What we were looking at, one woman explained, was part of a herd of centrosauruses, a six-metre-long ceratopsian, or horned dinosaur, with a head about a metre long and possibly dark hide (no one knows for sure what colour the dinosaurs were). Not far away was a bed of lambeosauruses. They had something paleontologists called a "head crest" on top of their skulls. From a distance, it made them look as though they had some sort of wild, slicked-back hairdo, kind of like Elvis in his prime. The head crest was hollow in spots and sometimes actually had nasal passages. The way they were put together allowed them to make a sort of trumpeting sound. Apparently another hadrosaur, one called a parasaurolophus, gave out such a spectacular noise that it sounded as if it were blowing a trombone through the back of its head.

I made a comment about the lambeosaurus being amazing.

"That's nothing," said the woman. "There's a dinosaur that had two brains. One was in its hips."

They let us do some digging. We all got down on our haunches, even Newcombe and Ophelia. Me and the guys tried to be very gentle at our work at first (not wanting to bust a seventy-five-million-year-old fossilized bone in half), but Dorothy just started hacking away. I guessed she had done this before.

Newcombe was duded up like he thought he was Indiana Jones, wearing a brown leisure-suit jacket over a white shirt with those pocket pens; beige shorts that showed his knobby, hairy knees; black knee-socks under his work boots; and a sort of safari hat that made him look like what we called a "double-idiot." He had that big briefcase with him and at one point he pulled a huge umbrella out of it, a parasol, and planted it in the ground near his work station for shade. Ophelia, a "triple-idiot," was wearing a dress. It actually looked like a dress, too, one you might wear to a ball or something. And you could smell the perfume on her. Dorothy, of course, was also wearing one, but it was way different: a flowery, summer dress sort of thing with these black tights underneath and a baseball cap on backwards with three pigtails sticking out various holes. Funny thing about her...she didn't seem to sweat.

We worked for about an hour or two, carefully clearing the dirt away from the bones. It was amazing to think about what we were doing: unearthing the corpses of these ancient beasts.

"These dinosaurs would be pounding and plodding around here in herds," enthused Hadrosaur-man, "eating leaves or needles off giant trees, always listening for the sudden, violent appearance of an albertosaurus, or maybe a pack of raptors. Up above them there might be pre-historic birds, some like gigantic vultures with wingspans twice the length of your car." He was getting all worked up again, big kid that he was, but I didn't blame him. It would have been truly wicked.

When it was time to leave we all got up and stretched. We thanked the paleontologists and began walking away. That was when Terry stumbled on something no more than a few strides from the bone bed. He leaned down and picked it up. It was a bone, left intact.

"Whoa," said Rhett quietly, walking up to him.

"What is it?" asked Bomber, his eyes bulging. "A T. rex? A triceratops?"

"Too small for that," said Newcombe, coming forward. "Much too small. And besides, it isn't fossilized. It's an actual bone."

Both Hadrosaur-man and the woman paleontologist had noticed our discovery and walked towards us. As we stood around looking at it, they were silent.

Finally, Newcombe turned to them. "I don't recognize this. Do you?"

"Uh, yeah," said the woman.

"And?"

"It's from an animal that died very recently," she said grimly.

"Recently?" asked Ophelia, a bit startled.

"And its owner was about twelve or thirteen years old."

"Thirteen years old? What kind of animal is it, then?" said Newcombe.

"It's, uh…a human being."

As Terry dropped the bone, Ophelia fainted. She did a bit of a spiral as she fell, rolled over once, and landed right on the herd of lambeosauruses.

5

A CHANGE OF PLANS

It took five minutes to revive Ophelia, though it seemed like about half an hour. They were waving things in front of her face, trying to fan some oxygen into her, and Newcombe was whining away, saying, "Come back to me, baby," or something sick like that. Finally, they brought out an all-terrain vehicle and lugged her onto it and we all went back to the museum.

But we didn't stay there for long. Soon we were driving into town. We hadn't been planning on staying in Dinosaur Hall that night and if we had been, I think Newcombe would have cancelled it. He was glad to get Ophelia away from bones of any sort. That being said, the name of our new digs, the Jurassic Inn, hardly made you think of home sweet home.

Newcombe didn't say too much during the trip back, but you could tell he was thinking about things, very seriously. His jaw muscles were tight and his teeth were grinding away as if he were trying to sculpt them into something.

As soon as Bomber and Rhett were checked into their room, they headed over to mine and Terry's, and we got down to the business of figuring out what the heck that human bone was doing at the dig site. But before we were really into it, there was a knock at the door. It was Dorothy.

"Didn't think I'd let you guys have all the fun, did you?" she cracked, bouncing into the room.

"So, what do you think?" I asked.

"I think you guys are goners. You can kiss your dinosaur adventures goodbye."

That was a depressing possibility—not something we wanted to think about.

"What about the human bone? Where do you think that came from?" asked Bomb.

"Beats me. I know there have been kids lost in the badlands. Lost and never found."

"So that's it," said Rhett.

"But that's not what Newcombe's thinking," said Terry quietly. "He thinks that bone is very recent. Like, from this week. He thinks it has something to do with the Reptile."

"Maybe it does," I said, taking the words out of Dorothy's mouth.

"Well," she said dryly, "if it does, then it's probably the most exciting thing that's ever happened in Drum." That was the second time today she had said something like that. She seemed to think her hometown was a pretty boring place. Didn't she know that she lived in Oz?

"I'll bet this sort of thing happens in Toronto all the time."

There was a pause.

"Uh, not really," said Terry. "If it did, we'd move."

"It doesn't matter where it usually happens," I said. "What matters is that here, right now, we have a human bone lying in the sand just a short walk from the Royal Tyrrell Museum. And it didn't drop from the sky. The way I see it, we have two missions in front of us. One is to find out where that bone came from, and the second is to convince Newcombe that it has nothing to do with the Reptile."

There was a knock on the door.

"Boys?" said a whiny voice from the other side.

It was Newcombe, likely about to kill both our missions. Bomb started to call out to him to come in when Dorothy slapped her hand over his mouth. Oh, yeah. Girls weren't allowed in our room. If Newcombe had found her, we might have been on a plane home that night.

Dorothy stood up and frantically paced, searching for a hiding place. The door started to open. She darted under the bed. No time for new ideas.

"Boys..." started Newcombe. He noticed us all sitting up very straight, likely looking more than a little guilty. We weren't exactly international men of mystery.

"Uh...is everything all right?" He started glancing around.

"Fine, sir, everything's fine," I said. My voice, unfortunately, cracked a little on the first word, making me sound as though I were about five years old.

"Well," said Newcombe, still looking a little suspicious and walking around the room, peeking behind doors as he spoke. "I have come to a conclusion."

"Which is?" said Terry, wanting the news out.

"Which is that we will spend two more days here and then we will go home."

There was a collective groan. But Newcombe was having none of our protest.

"I am not changing my mind. Mrs. Newcombe had a terrible fright today. And so did I, it must be admitted. I'll be honest with you all. There is a horrible criminal on the loose in this province, and it seems likely that he is in our very midst."

"That's kind of cool though, isn't it, sir?" That was Bomb. And it was a very lame thing to say. It was as if he'd suffered a brain lapse or something (he has those every now and then) and figured he was talking to another thirteen- or fourteen-year-old for a second.

"No, it isn't cool."

We all laughed. We just had to. Norris Newcombe saying "cool" was just a killer thing to hear, worth the whole trip.

He had a puzzled look on his face as he continued.

"I cannot ensure your safety under these circumstances, nor protect my wife from harm. I am equipped with knowledge of jiu-jitsu and a little kung fu, and if I were to find this Mr. Reptile fellow myself, I would administer a sound beating to him and let him know of his evil ways. But I cannot protect you all."

We all laughed again. Now he looked more angry than puzzled.

"Two more days. That's it. I had to bargain with Mrs. Newcombe to even get that much. I had to promise her that we would venture out for only the safest of field trips and that all of you would be near us every moment. On the third day, we will be heading home. I will be speaking with your parents this evening."

The parental units are pretty out of it—they couldn't really help that, being their age and all. But even they thought Newcombe was a head case. I'd have loved to hear that conversation.

Newcombe vanished out the door, and Dorothy reappeared.

"Two days, kiddies," she said.

"If only we could flush out this Reptile guy and let Newcombe lay a little of that kung fu on him," I said, barely able to get it out as we all burst into laughter again.

"Yeah," said Terry, "maybe Newcombe could use his face to soften up the guy's fists."

But our laughter didn't last. We were all bummed out about having our trip cut short.

"We can't let this happen," said Bomb.

"We don't have any choice," replied Rhett.

"Yes, you do," said Dorothy. "We can try to find this guy."

"Are you nuts?" asked Terry.

"Of course I am," she said. "Only way to be. Hunting him down would be like something from the movies, like something that never happens in Drum."

"I think you have something wrong there," said Terry. "He's the hunter. Not us. In real life, we don't stand a chance."

The room was quiet again. I looked over at Dorothy. She seemed sort of embarrassed, as if she had said something childish. I wanted to make some comment to defend her idea, but it really didn't make any sense. Our best plan was to enjoy the next two days and hope that the Reptile would go away.

"Maybe they'll catch him in a couple of days," said Terry. "Or maybe they'll find evidence that he's somewhere else."

"Well," I said, "they've got that bone down at the RCMP office right now, so we'll likely hear something about it pretty soon. Or let's put it this way: *they'll* know something about it—whether they tell *us* or not is another matter. If it's connected to the Reptile in any way, then this place is going to be pretty shook up, and we might be *lucky* to get two more days. Let's make the best of what we have."

And so we agreed to keep our chins up.

Soon, Dorothy took off for home, and then Bomber and Rhett, a little late, tiptoed back to their room. When they were all gone, Terry and I got ready for bed, put the lights out, and climbed in. He is usually a great guy to talk with, being a brain and all that, but on this night he just drifted off to sleep.

I was wide awake. I got up and walked over to the window. I could see the outline of the hills of the badlands in the distance. In the darkness the whole place looked even spookier. Suddenly I saw a light, like a torch, go on and then off, way out in the distance. It could have been anything, I suppose. But I just had a feeling about this place. I couldn't shake that sense that someone was watching us. And Terry was right. If there was going to be a hunt of any sort, we were going to be the prey.

6

A REPTILE NEARBY

Dorothy Osborne never stopped believing that we could do something about the Reptile. But at first she didn't say anything. For a while, after Terry made that movie comment, she stopped talking about the subject entirely. I could see her thinking, though.

The Reptile story was all over the weekly *Drumheller Mail* the next day, with pictures of the ugly beanpole himself leering out at us. And everyone in town was talking, too. The articles didn't say anything about the human bone. Obviously, the police wanted that kept quiet. People were freaked out enough as it was. Everyone was told to remain calm—everything was under control. But we knew it wasn't. And that was the last time we heard anything about the bone for a while.

Our "itinerary," as Newcombe liked to put it, called for us to make a little trip along the Dinosaur Trails west of Drumheller that day. There were some tourist attractions and a few other things we could see. The trip had originally included a long hike into a place called Horsethief Canyon with our sleeping bags and packs for an overnight stay under the stars deep in the badlands. Newcombe, of course, had put a stop to that, under the influence of the quivering Ophelia. But we all whined and complained so much about it that he agreed to ask the RCMP if they would send an officer with us so we could at least go on some of the hike.

So, that was how Constable Steele Lougheed ended up as one of our happy campers that day. He was quite a picture, with his rock jaw and perfectly combed black hair and his habit of putting on a white Stetson whenever he got out of his vehicle. A nice man, but about as easy to interrogate as James Bond. Dorothy cornered him a few times and asked him about the human bone—well, you would have thought she was talking about something from a fairy tale. The first time she mentioned it, he said he had no idea what she was talking about. "That's the first I've heard of it," he said, and smiled. The second time she asked him, he said *exactly* the same thing. That seemed more than a little suspicious.

Anyway, he was as nice a host as you could imagine. He even told Newcombe he'd take all of us along the Dinosaur Trails in his RCMP van. So off we went, Mr. Rock Jaw behind the wheel. Ophelia was more than a little impressed, and she blushed when he tipped his hat to her and assured her that the Mounties always got their man, and that she had nothing to fear from this desperado.

"Ma'am," he said, "we will protect you, I'll stake my reputation on it." Dorothy kind of gagged at that one, but I thought it was sort of neat, in a way.

Constable Lougheed also had a horse, called Flame. He was grooming it in a little stable behind the police headquarters near the rink when we got there. Ophelia was more than a little impressed with that, too. She even let slip that she thought Constable Lougheed might soon track down the Reptile on his mighty steed. Now that I'd have liked to see.

We started along the South Dinosaur Trail, heading west, out of town, near the southern bank of the Red Deer River. At first it was pretty unspectacular. There were just a lot of warehouses and gas stations and that sort of thing. But then we saw Jesus. There he was, in a field in the distance. Someone had made a huge cross and put his image on it. It towered over the badlands. I found it a little spooky, to be honest. Not many towns have a seven-foot Jesus hanging around on their outskirts, watching over things as though they need protection from God.

They must be awfully religious in Drumheller, because our next stop, just a minute or so later, was at the site of a play, a "Passion Play," they called it. Here, for a few weeks every summer, thousands of people fill huge rows of stands built into the badlands to see a reenactment of the death of Jesus. We could see the nearby hills where He gets crucified. I imagined the thousands watching, looking out over a place that probably looks a lot like the land where He actually lived long ago.

"They have a cast of hundreds," said Constable Lougheed in a very serious voice, hand on his gun, as if he might just have to unload a round into anybody who wasn't God-fearing or law-abiding enough.

We walked right out onto the stage, which had stone walls to represent buildings from two thousand years ago.

"What a great spot for the Reptile to hide," said Dorothy, whispering into my ear. "He could bed down in one of these fake buildings. Who'd look for him here?"

She was right. After that, I watched my back. Every door that creaked open made my head dart around. Every shadow that moved made me start. But if he was there, he kept himself well hidden. I looked back through the rear window of the van as we pulled out, examining every opening in the stone walls.

Dorothy was sitting in the seat directly in front of me, her face almost pressed against a window. That comment about the Reptile was the only thing she had said since we'd left that morning. She stared out at the countryside as though she were looking for something.

As the main road veered off straight west, we turned and headed northwest, right into the heart of the valley. Our road was only a few metres from the river. Soon we began to climb, and the Red Deer fell away below us. Up we went, as if we were scaling a mountain. We reached the top, and Constable Rock Jaw turned onto a dirt path. "Orkney Viewpoint," read a sign. We came to a stop.

I couldn't believe what we saw next. Dorothy obviously knew what to expect because she suddenly became excited and raced out of the van. For a few seconds it looked as if she were trying to commit suicide. She ran directly towards the edge of a cliff, and when she got there, she jumped off…and disappeared! More than a little shocked, I rushed to the edge and looked straight down. And there was Dorothy, grinning up at me, crouching in some bushes on the other side of this massive hill we were on. She had quite a flair for the dramatic!

"Thought I was a goner, eh?" She laughed. "No way! Did you ever see *Rebel Without a Cause*? I just love old movies. These two guys have this game of chicken where they drive their cars off the edge of a cliff. One of them gets out alive, James Dean, but the other one doesn't. And *his* girlfriend, played by Natalie Wood, runs up to the edge and peers over with this horrified look on her face. Like *you* just did."

"Thanks," I said.

Up above us, Bomb, Terry, and Rhett were saying "wicked" and "cool" and all those things we say when something really wicked and cool turns up. They were staring out into the distance.

Newcombe was about as emotional as he ever gets. "My, my, what a truly wonderful view!" he exclaimed. Then he put his arm around Ophelia and she beamed up at him, which just about gagged us all again.

Dorothy stood up and turned around. "Best view in Canada, I'll bet," she said.

Stretching out before us was what looked like just about all of southern Alberta, with the blue-brown Red

Deer River flowing through it, the badlands framing everything, and the beginnings of Drumheller like some sort of toy town in the distance. Close to the river the land was green, and we could see tiny specks that were cattle, grazing. The drop beneath us was very steep, though there were paths leading downward. It was really stunning. It reminded me of scenes in old westerns, like *Butch Cassidy and the Sundance Kid* or something like that, when the outlaws are being chased, and they head to higher ground and get up on some sort of mountain and look back at the posse that's after them. They see these little spots, maybe clouds of dust, slowly bearing down on them. So off they go again, as fast as they can.

It was another view that looked like a painting. There seemed to be a lot of those around here. But this one was beautiful, just beautiful, and that isn't a word I throw around very often.

We must have all stood there for about five or ten minutes without speaking again. Then me and the guys tried to see how far we could fire rocks into the valley. Most of them didn't even make it down the hill. We decided to heave some bigger rocks, and then Bomb and Rhett thought they'd pick up Terry and launch him over the edge, too. At that moment Newcombe said it was time to go.

I turned for one last look.

"He's out there somewhere," I heard a voice whisper in my ear.

I wished she would stop doing that.

Ten minutes later, the road started twisting around and then descended to the river. This was where the South Dinosaur Trail ended and the North began. It was also the location of what had to be the world's shortest boat ride. The Bleriot Ferry is just a raft, really, and it ferries people across a spot in the river that is only about five times the boat's length. You drive your vehicle on, the ferry floats at about one kilometre per hour for about two seconds, and then you drive off. I'm into history, but that seemed a bit much. A bridge, guys? How about just a tiny little bridge here?

Anyway, Constable Rock Jaw drove us off, waved to the ferry captain (now *that* has to be a boring job), and started whipping up this winding road on the other side of the river, up into the hills of the badlands again. He drove about a million clicks an hour. I suppose he didn't have to worry about speeding tickets.

In a few minutes the road levelled off and we turned east to take the North Dinosaur Trail back to Drumheller. That was when we started seeing giant birds in the flat fields—and I mean giant. They were way bigger than human beings. Or at least that's what it looked like. They were massive vultures of some sort, pecking at the ground. Quetzalcoatluses back from the grave. But right away, Terry knew what they were.

"There's oil in them thar hills," he said.

"Oil, that is!" snapped Bomber.

"Black gold!"

"Texas tea!" shouted Rhett.

"And up from the ground came a bubblin' crude!" we all sang and then launched into the theme song for *The Beverly Hillbillies.* Dorothy actually smiled. But Ophelia looked at us as if we were quadruple idiots. No sense of humour, that woman.

What we were seeing were these machines they have for pumping oil out of the ground. If you take a drive into the right area of the province, you'll see them everywhere, bobbing their big metal heads up and down, plucking that oil out of the rich Alberta ground. They actually call them "donkeys," but they sure looked like giant birds to us.

We were in another one of those stretches that we'd seen when we first started out from Calgary, an area where the land was as flat as a pancake and farm buildings sat in the distance, though this looked more like cattle country than crop land. I could just imagine a cowboy on horseback in these parts, driving his herd. As I was thinking about that, Rock Jaw slowed the van and turned off the road. "Horsethief Canyon," said a sign. This was it! This was where we were going hiking! Reptile or no Reptile.

It was really a series of canyons, and the whole thing looked deeper and wider than Horseshoe. The sign said that in the late nineteenth and early twentieth centuries ranching was a big thing around here, and horses used to just vanish into these canyons. You knew your own horses in those days by their brands, and often when one disappeared into Horsethief it would reappear some time later with a different brand. That's how the canyon got its name.

"Yu know what yu get for stealin' horses, don't yu, pardner?" said Terry.

"No," said Bomber.

"Hangin'!" said Rhett.

"Or death by being thrown into a canyon!" said Terry, and they all tried to grab me and fire me over the cliff.

"BOYS!" cried Ophelia. I'd never heard her shout like that. She seemed really nervous.

"Only, uh, kidding, Mrs. Newcombe," said Terry quietly.

"There will be no kibitzing about!" proclaimed Norris, inching towards the edge of the cliff to peer over.

"Kib-what?" asked Bomber.

"Never mind. This is very dangerous country. We have exactly one hour here, and you will be under the command of Constable Lougheed." As he said this he got to the edge and peered down. His eyes looked as if they might roll up in their sockets and he seemed a little green in the face. He stepped back.

"Oh, 'command' seems a little stern, Mr. Newcombe," said Rock Jaw. "Let's let the boys have some fun here."

Maybe he wasn't going to be so bad after all.

He did lay down some rules, though. We could wander around a bit, but never out of easy earshot of the Mountie himself. And he would go down each cliff first, followed by us, with Newcombe bringing up the rear, so to speak. Anybody who saw anything suspicious was to report it immediately. No one was to touch snakes, scorpions, or any other crawling thing, and all sightings of such critters were to be reported as well.

"On your way down the hills make sure you have good footing for every step, or don't take that step... you could end up on your ass."

Ophelia did a little jump when he used that word.

"My apologies, ma'am," he said. "Quite right. I'm sure these boys never use language like that." He winked at me. "I meant to say that they could end up on their bums."

We all laughed out loud.

Ophelia wasn't going to land on *her* bum. No sir. She was staying behind. She was going to man the landing—*woman* it, to be more exact—and listen for any messages that might come through for Lougheed on the radio in the van.

We stood at the very edge—me, Bomber, Rhett, Terry, and Dorothy. The guys had this look of excitement in their eyes. Her expression was different. It was that distant look again. She scanned the horizon.

Horsethief Canyon had to be the coolest place I ever stood on the brink of, knowing that I was about to enter it. It was like starting out on a video game, except I would be part of it. *Trek Through the Badlands,* or something like that.

"*Search for the Reptile,*" said a voice in my head. I turned around and saw Dorothy up close, looking at me. Had she really said that?

I turned back to Horsethief. Off to the right there was a massively deep, dead-end canyon; over to the left, another one; and then in the middle there was a wide one that went a long way and then turned. After it turned it was hard to tell where it went. It seemed to vanish into a whole series of other canyons and badlands that ranged off into the distance of the Red Deer River valley.

The sun was out and blazing. Everything was hot and dusty. The sky was a deep blue and far away, and there were huge black shadows in the canyons, hiding great stretches of terrain in all directions. It made you wonder what might lurk in there. The huge beehive hills were everywhere, with those coloured stripes running across their sides. Deep down, at the bottom of the canyons, there were flat areas of green grass and sand and little creeks that looked nearly dried up. Man, it made me want to dive right into it! As I looked way off into that main canyon below I could just imagine Butch and the Kid out there on horseback, pursued by the bad guys...or the good guys, I guess it was.

Of course, we had a Mountie with us. He would have just ridden out there and nailed old Butch and Sundance, no fooling around.

"Ready?" asked Constable Rock Jaw.

Need he ask?

We went up to the edge and then down, straight down, into Horsethief Canyon.

On the way, several of us *did* land on our bums. One time I bounced off mine and kept on going, down, for about ten metres. It was a little scary. For an instant I was worried that I wouldn't be able to put the brakes on at all and would just keep on falling all the way to the bottom of the canyon. I could tell the other guys were a little freaked out once or twice too, but no one said anything. You just can't. Dorothy didn't slip at all. I chalked that up to experience.

I couldn't believe how steep it was, like walking down the side of a sheer cliff. And the ground was very different from what I had imagined it would be. It was sandy and slippery. It had rained recently, and that made the footing particularly treacherous. Before long we were all going very slowly indeed.

Every time it seemed like we were at the bottom, we'd realize that we had farther to go. We'd come to a flat area and walk along it for a while, and then down we'd go again. Whenever I turned to see where we had been, I was amazed by how far up I had to look. The lookout, where the van was, seemed to be straight up from us and a million metres high. I started wondering how we were going to get back out. By donkey? Helicopter?

But there was something so cool about it. The guys all had pretty serious looks on their faces but I could tell they were loving it. Here we were, descending into some sort of alien landscape, and yet we were fifteen minutes from our hotel in Drumheller. If we only had some guns and ammo, like in video games, could we ever get it on!

Finally, we got to the very bottom. Everything was flat, and the hills loomed above us. Bomber, Terry, and I started running beside a little creek on the sandy soil. We ran with everything we had. It was amazing to be able to do that down there. We were letting off steam, too, I guess. Dorothy and Rhett stood back and watched us. Newcombe didn't seem to care, seemed to understand for once. I think we all had this dangerous idea that we'd like to just run and run and run, until we got lost in this fantastic land. But when we were about a hundred metres away, it became too much for Newcombe, and he yelled to us. We circled around and came back.

Constable Rock Jaw was talking.

"You know there are lots of legends about the badlands, many from as far back as when the Blackfoot and Peigan ruled here. They believed, for example, that dinosaur bones were the remains of ancient buffalo;

other Indigenous people said they were evidence of prehistoric giants. And you know, in the Bible it talks about giants running the world long ago. But the legend I like best is about the dinosaur that's still around."

"What?" said Newcombe, rather impolitely for him, I thought.

"Yep. Some scientists think the descendants of dinosaurs are still with us in the form of birds. Apparently, if you look at the way a bird is put together, you pretty well have a dino. But this is much spookier than that. Over the years a legend has grown that there are animals somewhere deep in the badlands that look almost *exactly* like actual dinosaurs. No one has ever seen them, but fresh footprints have been found. Or so it's said. There's lots of speculation about what they look like and why people never see them. Story is... they're a sign of evil."

"Evil?" said Newcombe.

"How big are they supposed to be?" I asked.

"Little guys. Tiny dinosaurs keeping away from all us big mammals, like the tables have been turned since the Cretaceous period."

"You know, the idea that dinosaurs never became extinct actually makes some sense to me," said Dorothy. "I understand the bird thing, but what if it went even further than that? What if there are dinosaurs that look like dinosaurs hiding away somewhere where no one ever sees them?"

"Yeah," said Terry. "I mean, obviously certain animals can become extinct, but who ever heard of an entire species just vanishing like that, overnight? If the birds are still around, then why aren't there actual dinosaurs, too?"

"Because they were killed off by a sudden change in climate," said Newcombe dryly, "perhaps brought on by a huge asteroid hitting the earth. Its debris blocked out the sun, cooled off the climate, and killed all the plants so the plant-eaters had nothing to eat. When the plant-eaters started dying, the meat-eaters starved as well."

"That's just a theory," snapped Dorothy.

Newcombe looked shocked. She had dismissed his pearls of wisdom.

"Scientists have been wrong before," agreed Bomber. "And they all admit that they don't know for sure what happened. Dorothy's right. It's just a theory."

Now Newcombe looked kind of peeved.

"So, maybe the dinosaurs just evolved backwards," I said. "Maybe they became fewer and fewer, and smaller and smaller."

"Right," said Dorothy, holding her hand to her forehead to shield the sun, so she could see me. She was smiling.

"Fantasy!" Newcombe shot back at us, with a sort of smirk on his face. "Very unsound science, students."

"Man," rumbled Rock Jaw, "I'd love to find me a miniature T. rex in one of these caves."

"Or a seven-foot one with a shaved head," said Dorothy. This time she didn't whisper. For a second there was silence. We all just stopped and looked at her.

"Let's move on," said Constable Lougheed. He glanced around as he spoke, up and down the sides of the hills. For some reason he had a slightly worried look.

Dorothy started talking a little more after that—she was becoming her old self again. Mostly she talked with me. She mentioned a few things about her friends and said that the group of girls I'd seen her with when we first came into town were pretty close and did everything together. "We like to dress a little different," she confided. "We're all getting out of Drumheller some day and making something of ourselves, escaping. We all want to be famous. We kind of run the Drama Society at school: me and Em, Reen, Hank, and Lou. We call ourselves 'the Famous Five.' You have to have big dreams."

"Can't you have dreams here?" I asked.

"You've got to be kidding!" She laughed.

We had turned the corner on the canyon floor and couldn't even see the lookout hill any more. It was kind of scary to see how similar everything seemed, how easy it would be to get lost. But something about it was kind of exciting, too.

"HOLD IT!" shouted Lougheed suddenly.

We all froze. He sounded serious.

"Hear that?" he asked.

We all shook our heads.

"Someone's calling."

He turned and walked back a few strides, retracing our footsteps.

"And it's coming from…" He stopped dead and listened. "Someone's in trouble!" he cried, and then he broke into a run. It didn't take more than a nanosecond for the rest of us to do the same.

"Keep up, boys! Keep up!" shouted Newcombe, as he fell behind all of us, his glasses falling off his sweaty nose as he ran. He kept pushing them back on and glancing all around in fear. He was "puffing like a steer," as I'd heard a cowboy in Drumheller say. But so were we. We were desperate to keep up to our Mountie. We rounded the corner and headed back up the canyon floor towards our starting point.

"HALT!" yelled Lougheed, holding up his hand and coming to such a sudden stop that we all almost knocked into him. He stood very still for a minute, as if listening to the wind.

Then I heard it. A tiny voice in the distance, almost swallowed up by the heat and the dust. Lougheed looked up, and when he did, so did I. He was gazing back to the exact spot, distant now, where we had parked the van. We could see a tiny figure standing on the top of the hill like a toy. We could see it frantically waving its hands and we heard that tiny voice again.

It was Ophelia. And she sounded frightened out of her mind. A feeling deep inside told me that we couldn't sneer at this. Ophelia wasn't just being paranoid again. Something had happened, something wild. We all broke into a run, as fast as we could go.

7

WHAT OPHELIA HEARD

It should have taken us at least an hour to climb back up the steep cliffs of Horsethief Canyon, but we just flew. All of us except Norris, of course. He was moaning things about "My baby, my baby" and stumbling and falling. At one point Rhett got behind him and kind of grabbed him by his big, broad butt and almost drove him up the hill.

When we got to the top, Ophelia could barely talk. She came running towards us like I'd never seen her run, her dress flapping around her knees. She stopped for an instant, looked at us, then glanced back and forth between Newcombe and Lougheed. Finally she threw herself into Rock Jaw's arms.

"Be calm," said the Mountie. "Take a deep breath and then speak slowly. Just tell us what's happened."

"The...the..." she stammered.

"Yes?" said Rock Jaw, calmly.

"The Reptile!" she gasped.

"Reptile?" said Lougheed, and even he turned a little white.

"Oh, my darling!" cried Newcombe, and he pried her from the Mountie's arms.

But Rock Jaw was on the job. He snatched her away, looked her dead in the eyes, and asked her to explain herself. We all gathered around them in a circle.

"There was a report...on your radio...that he's been seen!"

"Where?!" said Lougheed.

"In...in..."

"In where?" demanded Dorothy, her look riveted on Ophelia's quivering face, eyes as large as a dinosaur's.

"In...this...canyon."

And with that, she fainted again.

WE DROVE BACK TOWARDS DRUMHELLER along the North Dinosaur Trail, and the RCMP van barely seemed to touch the road. We zoomed past the Royal Tyrrell Museum, a Go-Kart place, a golf course in the desert, the "world's largest little church" (seats one thousand people, six at a time), and on into town. When we landed at the RCMP offices near the arena, Lougheed leapt out and ordered us all to "Disembark!" We were to walk back to the Jurassic Inn. He was going to load his horse into a trailer and return to the canyon. Apparently, there was already a whole battalion or detachment (or whatever they're called) on its way from Calgary.

We picked up our stuff at the Jurassic Inn and headed over to another place where we were scheduled to stay for a couple of days. Because of the whole Reptile thing and Newcombe's paranoid reaction to it, the new plan was to stay there one night and then do something very safe the next day before heading for Calgary and home in the evening. One day left. We probably wouldn't even know if they caught the guy. What fun was that?

It was almost dinnertime, so Dorothy had to go home. She left with this anxious expression on her face, like the one you get when the power goes out right in the middle of a cliffhanger of a TV show. She didn't say a word, but I knew what she was thinking: *You know we should go after the Reptile. You know we should be part of this.*

Me and the guys didn't talk about the situation as we packed. Newcombe wouldn't have allowed it. He got all our stuff, and us, into the van and carefully strapped in Ophelia, who wasn't quivering any more—she was just kind of staring off into space.

We were pretty charged up about the fact that this desperado was right in our midst.

"Imagine," whispered Terry once we were on our way, "he was right there!"

"I thought it felt like someone was watching us," said Bomber.

"Right, Bomb," laughed Rhett. "You knew all along."

"I didn't say that. I just had a weird feeling."

"Who doesn't?" I said.

"Now we know how the plant-eaters felt when old T. rex was stalking them," said Terry.

This new place was a "bed and breakfast"—in other words a house, an old one, with lots of what Newcombe called "character." Actually, it was pretty cool. It was right downtown, a three-storey building with a nice big verandah and little round windows on the top floor. Turns out it was originally the home of Jesse Gouge, which was a good name for him because he was one of the first mine owners in the area and a guy who made a load of bucks by getting other people to dig coal out of the ground for him. And those little windows on the top floor? They were for Gouge's men to stick their rifles through in case of a violent miners' strike. I guess in the old days Drumheller more than *looked* like the Wild West.

The house was nearly a hundred years old and run by a retired couple who knew more about Dinosaur Valley than you could hold in a book. There were antiques all over the place and a beautiful, long dining-room table where we'd have breakfast in the morning. From the sounds of what we were to be served, it was going to be one heck of a giant Alberta meal: hot cereal and pancakes and sausages and French toast, all done up with fresh fruit and whipped cream.

"Taste the Past" was the name of the place, and that seemed about right—it made you feel like you'd gone back in time. And the people who ran it were so friendly that Ophelia soon started to calm down. They sat us around their kitchen table and we began to talk.

"The first thing to think about is why this Reptile fellow would even come to these parts," said Clark Aberhart. He was the husband half of the team that ran the house, a solid sort who had travelled all over Canada and seemed to love every inch of it. But he loved Drumheller the most, and told some great stories, especially about the hermits who legend said lived in the badlands caves, and about those ghostly little dinosaurs. His wife, Faye Ray, was just as neat. She wore silk scarves and dresses and seemed more like a movie star than an artist. But that's what she was—she painted in a studio behind the house and her art was on the walls all over the place.

"It's obvious," she said, finishing Clark's thoughts, as she often did, "that the Reptile is trying to flee. You can vanish into the badlands like no other place in Alberta."

"But he is also a vicious criminal," said Ophelia.

"Who wants everyone to leave him alone," responded Clark. "He isn't looking for contact with people."

"In fact, he's trying to make sure he doesn't even leave a trace," said Faye Ray. "Leave him alone and he'll leave you alone. Just stay where there are lots of people and let the Mounties handle this. You are as safe as houses here."

Soon the conversation turned to less frightening things—the Aberharts started telling us about Drumheller history. First they told us about the Blackfoot Confederacy that ruled these parts many centuries ago, and the Blood, Cree, and Peigan people. A white man named Henday came out this way in the 1750s and met the Cree chief. He was amazed when he encountered him because it was in a huge lodge and the chief greeted him while sitting on a massive, pure-white buffalo robe. About a century later, when Captain John Palliser visited, he saw the buffalo roaming in huge herds all over the land.

People from everywhere started coming to Alberta in the 1890s in a mass migration that lasted for two decades. Before that, really only a handful of settlers had come, and the Mounties, of course, who had trekked out there on horseback to establish a fort in 1874. That was something I just loved imagining.

It wasn't until the twentieth century began that anybody other than the Indigenous people lived in the local badlands. In those days they were considered evil lands that were of no use, cursed by the gods. A guy named Thomas Greentree moved his family there in 1902, into a log cabin he put up on a flat spot near the Red Deer River about a slapshot from where the arena and that giant tourist dinosaur are now. He was a cattle rancher. One day, an American from Washington State showed up at his cabin, in the snow, looking for land. Greentree wasn't home, but this guy opened the door and went right in anyway—there were different rules in those days. He couldn't believe what he saw inside. Greentree had an unusual way of heating his home: there was an entire bucket of almost pure coal near the fireplace. In minutes the American was stomping around in the snow outside, and he soon found a seam of coal more than a metre wide in a hill. It didn't take him long to get back to Calgary, stake some mineral rights, and rush back.

When he returned, it was by car—no small feat in those days. Some think he followed old prairie trails, got horses to pull him up hills, and then drove up the river on the ice. He yanked $2,800 out of his shirt pocket and bought all sorts of land from Greentree.

Before long—between this guy, Jesse Gouge, and others—the biggest coalfield in Canada was in operation. Soon there would be more than one hundred mines, and men and women coming from all over the world to break their backs working to make their owners rich.

By 1911 the area needed a name. Tom Greentree thought he might call it "Greentree's Crossing." But he figured it only fair to give the American who had bought so much land a shot at naming it. So they flipped a coin to decide. The American won. His name was Sam Drumheller.

That was twenty-seven years after Joseph Tyrrell found that giant lizard skull, his *Albertosaurus sarcophagus*, near Kneehill Creek, evidence of a fantastic creature that roamed the area before human beings even existed. And after Lawrence Lambe had visited— the man whose name would be given to those big lambeosauruses, the beasts whose bones we had seen… and Ophelia had done a nosedive onto.

Whenever I heard stories about the past, I often wondered about something that I guess didn't make a lot of sense. I wondered where it had all gone. Where was that Cree chief who sat on the white buffalo robe? The buffalo themselves, that had pounded through the flat lands here like thunder? And where were all those dinosaurs—T. rex, triceratops, and albertosaurus? Bigger than elephants, made of armour, lethal, and ruling the world—gone as if they'd never existed. How could they all just go away? It was truly hard to believe. Maybe those last little dinosaurs had simply just refused to disappear.

NEWCOMBE LOOKED MUCH MORE relaxed by the time we were ready for bed, mostly because Ophelia was feeling better. He gathered us in their room, the largest of the three we were using, and announced that the next day, our last, was actually going to be a "big one." He had decided that in the morning we would take in a few sights east of the town—in other words, on the side where the

Reptile wasn't—and then we would drive about 150 kilometres southeast to Dinosaur Provincial Park. The Reptile would be but a distant memory there, and this park, according to Newcombe, was the king of dinosaur lands, a World Heritage Site that would, in his words, "knock us out." It would at least be an exciting ending to our shortened trip.

So when we went to sleep that night, in the antique beds of Taste the Past, we actually had something to dream about. There was only one day left, but we were going to make the most of it. Newcombe had made this provincial park thing sound interesting. He'd become so excited talking about it that his glasses had started to fog up, and Ophelia was glowing at him again.

"You can, and may, pick up dinosaur fossils all over that wonderful place," he'd said. "I guarantee you will find some. *That* is the area, not Drumheller, where scientists have discovered the most fossils of any spot in Canada. There are places in Dinosaur Provincial Park where they have found huge herds of these extraordinary beasts. When you get there, gentlemen, you will truly be in the bone beds of the badlands."

He'd made everything sound so perfect. But that always worried me. I put more trust in my dreams. Whole worlds and amazing stories always came to me when I slept, and they often seemed to tell me something about what was going to happen in my life. It was weird.

A dream entered my mind again as I slept that night, and it wasn't a good sign, not good at all. It was the T. rex with the Reptile's head again…and this time he finished the job…he ate me alive.

DOWN THE HIGHWAY, DEEP *in the canyon under the moonlight, the tall man was at work again. He carefully ground one footprint into the sand, then he removed both his boots. After each barefooted step, he carefully covered his print over with sand. It was masterfully done. One single footprint remained, far behind. Soon he came to a patch of grass. He replaced his boots and began moving again at a quick pace, using his long strides, sticking to the grass. He turned a corner and vanished, like a giant ghost…with a grin on its face.*

8

FOOTPRINTS

Dorothy got into the van the next morning looking like a cat that had swallowed a canary—a big canary. Something was up. I could hardly wait to ask her. She was wearing khaki pants and hiking boots, a light dress of about fifty colours tied around her waist, an army shirt, and a purple baseball cap. There was a big silver canteen slung over one of her shoulders. She sat at the back of the vehicle and kind of looked at me like she wanted me to sit with her. So I did. Once we were rolling east of Drumheller, past little Greentree Mall and some schools, she spilled the beans.

The night before, she had sneaked over to RCMP headquarters. Some of the officers had been returning from a long, hot day searching in Horsethief Canyon, and word was out that Corporal Lance "Lanny" Sutter had been sent in from Calgary. Dorothy crouched down low and made her way around the building to Constable Lougheed's office at the rear. She gambled that he might have his window open, to let in some of the fresh night air. She was right: it was wide open. And there were voices.

"Not a single sighting of him, sir," said Lougheed.

"But he's seven feet tall! How can we lose him?"

"The badlands is a big area, sir."

"So is Calgary, and if he were in Calgary we'd have him by now."

"Yes, sir, things are always bigger and better in Calgary."

"Was that sarcasm, Lougheed?"

"Of course not."

"How about that bone you found? Anything on it yet?"

"Not much, sir."

"Not much? Have you tried to match it with profiles of children who have disappeared in this area, or elsewhere in Alberta?"

"There's no need for that, sir."

There was a pause.

"No need?"

"We doubt, sir, that it even belonged to a child."

"We do?"

"Well, it's the right shape and size, and the right weight, but once the paleontologist on site took more than a glance at it she knew that there was something funny about it. In fact, she knew it wasn't human. Our people agreed, too. We're sending it to Toronto for more testing."

"Toronto? Everything is always bigger and better there, I suppose."

"Yes, sir."

"So, here's what we have: a seven-foot killer on the loose who has vanished into the sands, and the leg bone of a child that isn't the bone of a child at all."

"That's not quite all, sir."

"What do you mean?"

"Well, he seems to be able to cover his tracks very well. It's like following a ghost. But we did find one footprint."

"As in...a *single* footprint? How do you leave *one* footprint?"

"By being very clever, I'd say, sir. And wanting to toy with your pursuers. It was at the eastern end of Horsethief Canyon and it was pointing east, too."

"You mean, back towards Drumheller?"

"And Rosedale and Wayne and Dorothy and all those little tourist places east of town. He might be heading that way. We have no evidence he's been there before, and he's apt to seek new ground. But that's all speculation. After all…we only have one footprint."

"Yes. That isn't much to build a theory on, is it?" Sutter paused again. "Any *real* idea about what's going on here, Lougheed?"

"Not a clue, sir. But I do know something."

"What's that?"

"I'll catch him, if it's the last thing I do."

"Well, if you do catch up to this maniac, on that historical horse of yours, it *might* be the last thing you do." He paused. "By noon tomorrow I want it announced that there will be a curfew on all children in the Drumheller area. None of them out after dark. Got that? This guy has a thing for killing kids."

At that point the boss peered out the window right over Dorothy's head.

"Don't believe in air conditioning, Constable?" he said, and Dorothy could smell his breath.

One minute later, after he'd pulled his head back in, she was scurrying around to the front of the building and hightailing it home, her head buzzing with new information. The Reptile was still very much on the loose. And if he was going anywhere, it was east of Drumheller...*exactly* where we were going.

"SO, WE MIGHT NOT BE HEADING out of danger at all," said Dorothy in a low voice, "we might be going right into it." She sounded pleased, and of course she had no intention of warning Newcombe. He was in full swing behind the wheel of the van, pointing out the sights to us, and Ophelia was just thrilled with the way he was describing them, so they didn't even clue in that we were whispering at the back. At least, not at first. Just after Dorothy finished, the other guys noticed us huddling and started to crowd around. That was when Newcombe peeked into his rear-view mirror.

"Something you care to share with the rest, Miss Osborne?"

Dorothy is a quick thinker. "No, sir," she said. "I was just adding a few things to what you were saying and didn't want to disturb you. Please go on."

Newcombe smiled. And resumed his travelogue.

Actually, the places we saw that morning were pretty interesting. First we came to a little village called Rosedale, and we spent some time there trying to walk across this steel footbridge that was built a long time ago for miners. There was a bit of wind, and this thing was swaying. It just about made you ralph up your dinner to walk out onto it, but of course we had to take a crack at it. Dorothy calmly strode across like it was nothing. Funny thing was, we'd read on a plaque nearby that in the old days it didn't even have sides on it, so it would have been twice as hard to walk across—more like a high-wire act than a stroll on a bridge. That would have been something!

Because Dorothy was just whipping all the way over to the other side and the guys were having trouble getting even partway out, I took it upon myself to make our team look a little better. Despite feeling the pukes with just about every step, I staggered all the way across. The bridge swayed each time I set my foot on it. When I got to the other side Dorothy was bent over, with her hands on her knees and her head down.

"What?" I said. "Trip over upset your tummy?"

She glanced up at me. There was a weird sort of glow in her eyes. When she looked down again, I looked too. There, in the sand, were some footprints leading to the bridge. They looked like they'd been made by cowboy boots. Large cowboy boots...*very* large.

"Whoever made those marks must have been a big man," said Dorothy.

"Possibly." Something was making me uneasy.

"How big would you say?"

"I have no idea."

"Way over six feet, Dylan?…Seven feet…do you think?"

I told myself that what she was thinking was pretty far-fetched. We walked back, me trying to put those footprints out of my mind, she thinking she might just get her chance to chase down a cold-blooded killer. As we approached the other side, Rhett was looking at me, and he had a big smile on his face. I guess Dorothy's comments were bugging me more than I knew.

"Look like you've seen a ghost, Maples. Maybe the barf ghost?"

I tried to give him a smirk but I don't think it was very convincing. As we stepped off, I looked down and felt a little relief.

"There aren't any footprints on this side," I whispered to Dorothy.

We got into the van and headed out. Once we were moving again, I started feeling a little better. Dorothy was obviously imagining things.

About ten minutes farther east, Newcombe pulled over at probably the most bizarre land formation I've ever seen in my life—that's after fourteen years of looking. They're called hoodoos and that rhymes with voodoos, and that makes a lot of sense. That's because they're freaky. To me, they're what rocks might look like in hell. Very cool. You are driving along the highway and you look north of the road and these *things* appear, some of them two or three times as tall as a human being, weirder than anything Harry Potter could dream up. And they're real! That was what was hard to believe at first.

To be more specific, they looked like the giant toadstools from *Alice in Wonderland.* Made of sand and rock, they were pillars with flat plates on top, like hats. We got out and started walking among them. The sign said they had been formed by ten thousand years of wind and water erosion. The softer rock that made up the pillar part had eroded and a hard, sandstone layer just above them hadn't, so it had formed a cap, "acting like an umbrella" sheltering the softer rock below. In time, it said, each hoodoo would collapse.

"Hooooooo! Dooooooo!" shouted Bomber running among them. "We need some tunes! Some gangsta rap!"

I doubted that Bomb had ever listened to gangsta rap in his life. But he was right. We could have used some radical music to go with this place. Who needed the Reptile when you had this? But the hoodoos made

me think about why he had come here. If you were
a weirdo with a dark view of things, this would be
perfect.

"Look at that," said Dorothy, quietly, pointing off
into the distance. She had spotted one that was very
tall, twice as tall as any of the others, and as slim as a
knife; its cap was huge and off to one side. "People call
it the Devil's Tower." I thought she was going to make
another Reptile comment, but she didn't. She didn't
have to.

Our next stop going east was at the site of one of the
140 mines that had once been in this valley. The shaft
tunnelled straight into a dark hill for about a kilometre.
It was black and kind of sinister looking. You could
enter one of the miner's houses, too. It wasn't even the
size of our bathroom at home. There was a letter there
that he had written to his wife back in Europe. "I miss
you so much my heart aches to have you near me," it
read. "Once you are with me in our new home I will
never again leave you.... Your loving husband."

"Gag me," said Rhett, reading over my shoulder.
Funny thing is, that sort of thing never "gagged" me.
I thought it was sad. I mean, these were dead people.
And it sort of seemed like he loved her forever now.
The parental units were always going on about the

importance of love. But I turned to Rhett and the guys and said, "Gag me, big time." Dorothy was watching me when I did it and looked like she knew I wasn't really saying how I felt. How did she do that?

But to be honest, mines weren't really my thing just then. I'd had a bad experience in one just a few months earlier when I'd almost been trapped underground in northern Ontario with my girlfriend…that is…my friend who is a girl, Wynona Dixon. So, mines kind of freaked me out, and I didn't want to go into this one. When Dorothy asked me why, I started out by mentioning Wyn's name. She stopped me before I went any further.

"Who's she?"

"A friend."

"A good friend?"

"Well…she texts me. As I was starting to say, we kind of had a funny experience together in Ontario when my dad—he's a lawyer—was working on a case. It was like something from a book; we found some hidden silver and helped catch a criminal. It was pretty amazing."

"Bet he wasn't much compared to the Reptile," said Dorothy, and she stalked off.

It was getting near noon, and Newcombe wanted us to eat at this place Clark Aberhart had recommended near Rosedale, so we doubled back a bit. It was in a tiny village named Wayne, and to get to it you had to turn off the road, right into some badlands hills, and because the creek there twisted like a snake through the canyon, you had to cross eleven bridges in about five minutes, some of them old and rickety.

This place was right out of the movies. There were two light-brown buildings attached to each other, the taller one called the Rosedeer Hotel and the other the Last Chance Saloon. And I mean saloon. Even though there were cars around and a bunch of motorcycles, it would have made more sense to see a hitching post and some horses. I almost expected Wyatt Earp and Billy the Kid to come strolling out the front door.

We went into the saloon to eat. Clark had recommended the buffalo burgers (there were still some herds on farms nearby). The building, put up in 1913, had a low ceiling, big posts, wall-to-wall wood, and a great big bar that seemed to be half the room. There was a jukebox, Calgary Stampede posters, cowboy hats, rifles and guns, snowshoes nailed to the ceiling, a buffalo skull, and country music playing softly. A sign said they sold beer in fruit jars. And, strangest of all, there was a little wooden frame on a wall...around six bullet holes!

But the people were as friendly as could be. The owner even came over to say hello. He looked just like a cowboy, and his handle was Grant Tyson. He told us stories about all the fights that used to happen in the old days when the miners drank beer here. They used to go outside to fight—come back in friends—then go out and fight again.

"We're ready for this Reptile guy, by the way," laughed Tyson. "If he wants a showdown, just bring him on!" That didn't really seem to me like something to joke about.

We had a long way to go to Dinosaur Provincial Park, and Newcombe wanted to be back in Calgary well before sundown for the flight home, so once we had wolfed down the buffalo burgers, we were off. (The parental units are basically vegetarians, but I wouldn't be a lettuce-eater for all the oil in Alberta—I'm a meat-eater.)

"Had my best horse stolen early this morning," said Tyson, out of the blue, as we got up to leave. "Went by the name of John Ware. He was tied up, and whoever grabbed him just ripped the reins right off the hitching post. Didn't even try to cut them. Strange. Never had that happen before."

Dorothy was looking at me. I could feel it.

SEVERAL KILOMETRES TO THE *east, out of sight of the highway, in the heat of a badlands day, a tall man dressed in black was riding a horse as fast as it could go, urging it forward. His legs were so long they seemed to almost touch the ground. A lather of sweat was forming on the horse's hide, and perspiration poured down the man's white, skeletal face. He had just stopped for a rest in a little tumbleweed ghost town. He didn't care about the heat. His mind was set on a plan. He was thinking that at some point he might need a hostage or two.*

WE MOVED ON FROM THE SALOON. The rest of our trip would be about an hour and a half, but just as we approached the end of the badlands, just before the highway climbed out of Dinosaur Valley, we were to look out for a village called…Dorothy.

Dorothy herself knew all about it. In fact, its very existence had given her her name. It was in a flat, tumbleweed stretch near the end of the valley, and it was one of those places you would miss if you blinked. An abandoned grain elevator stood unsteadily near the highway, its red paint weather-worn, and the words "The Alberta Pacific Grain Co. Ltd." written across it near the top. You could just feel the ghosts there. There was a deserted school with a weather vane creaking in the breeze and a saloon that hadn't seen a cowboy in many, many years. Newcombe drove among the buildings, his mouth hanging open a little. We came to two churches, side by side, empty. The paint had almost all peeled off. They looked ready to fall down.

"Let's not go in," said Ophelia.

But Dorothy had already undone her seatbelt and dashed outside. I couldn't let her go alone, so I jumped out, too.

"Students!" shouted Newcombe.

The door of one church wouldn't even move—it seemed to be boarded up from the other side—but the other building's entrance almost fell in when we shoved it. Someone seemed to have been in there recently. Inside, everything was a mess, just piles of broken old pews and dusty curtains falling down. We stepped carefully. Then we saw some charred wood in a pile, as if someone had recently had a fire in there. On the floor next to it, two letters had been carved into the boards. Dorothy knelt down and brushed away the ashes. "T. R." it read.

I felt a shiver go through me.

"*The Reptile!*" said Dorothy, in a sort of freaky whisper.

"No way," I snapped back. "It could just as easily mean...*Tyrannosaurus rex.*"

"Same thing," said Dorothy. She got up and headed towards the door.

Just before we entered the van she turned and cupped her hand over my ear. *"He's following us,"* she breathed.

The guys really gave me the gears about her whispering into my ear like that. They were winking at me and jabbing me and that sort of thing. I could have stopped it all by just telling them what she'd said. But I couldn't.

I didn't know what to do. If I told Newcombe what we'd seen and confessed that I was getting worried, we'd never get to Dinosaur Provincial Park, never see much of anything on this trip, and worst of all, Dorothy would think I was a wimp. So I kept my mouth shut. And I tried to act normal. Besides, there wasn't really any evidence for what Dorothy was thinking. She just wanted some adventure, so she was putting one and one together and getting three.

A few minutes later we were in ranch country. Those huge Alberta farmlands stretched out all around us. There were almost no trees, and you could see forever. The giant oil birds appeared again, pecking at the ground.

For a while this Reptile business faded into the distance and we all started talking. Really talking.

We settled in for the longest part of the trip. One of the reasons we changed subjects was that I kind of steered things in that direction. I was trying to keep Dorothy's mind off the idea that we should be hunting a dangerous killer, and I started by asking her questions about her life. By the time we turned and headed south on Highway 36 towards Dinosaur Provincial Park, Dorothy had told us quite a bit about herself.

Turned out her parents had been in the movie business when they first came to Drumheller, and they still were in a way. All kinds of films had been shot in Dinosaur Valley over the years, including some really famous ones. Dorothy knew a lot about them: the first *Superman*, Clint Eastwood's killer cowboy flick *Unforgiven*, the western *Draw* with Kirk Douglas, kids' shows like *The Boy Who Talked to Badgers*, and lots of science fiction stuff. In the late 1990s her dad had written a movie that was filmed in Dorothy. Her mom, who had been an actress, had come with him from Los Angeles. Dorothy was born here not long after that. And that's how she got her name.

"My parents are kind of weird," she said.

"Whose aren't?" I replied.

"Yeah, but mine ended up living here. They fell in love with this place. Mom said she wanted a simpler life and gave up acting. Weird. I never would have. Dad's a writer, and he wanted to live in a quiet place, too. He always says the valley just spooks him and tells him things, and he adores it. He writes books, a lot of them travel books, and now Mom works with the Alberta government, helping with all the movie shoots that happen in the badlands. But I wish they'd stayed in LA. I sure would have. Imagine, I could have grown up there! I'm going back some day to be in the movies, I hope. I'm definitely not staying here."

"This seems like a pretty cool place to me," I said.

"Well, since the Reptile showed up, it has been."

There were a bunch of things about her I couldn't understand. First, of course, was her fascination with this dangerous killer. But another was her attitude about where she lived—seemed to me it could be a gas living here. But Dorothy was always talking about other places. She had an imagination like I couldn't believe. She had a story for just about everything, and most of them were pretty dramatic. For instance, when I picked out a spot nearby on the map (I just love maps) named Medicine Hat, she launched into a tale that just about freaked us all out. And she said it was true, too.

Apparently, trains used to be the main way to get around the west if you were going any distance. In the summer of 1908 an engineer named Bob Twohey and his fireman, Gus Day, took a small train east from Medicine Hat towards the village of Dunmore in order to pick up another one and take it southwest to Lethbridge. Just a few kilometres along their journey they saw something terrifying. There in front of them was an oncoming train, with a headlight "like a burning wagon wheel," speeding right at them along the same track. But as they readied themselves to jump they heard the other train's whistle sound a warning blast for the curve they had just been on. It was as if the other engineer intended to go right through them. But he didn't. Instead, he went on by…on a non-existent track that ran beside them. All the coach lights were on and the crew members were silently waving as they passed. Then this phantom train and its ghostly passengers went off into the night towards Medicine Hat.

Twohey and Day, both sturdy, no-nonsense Albertans, didn't say a word to each other. But two weeks later they met by chance in town and had to get things off their chests. Twohey, it turned out, had just been to a fortune teller, who had told him he would be dead in a month. He had been anxious to take some time off. Somewhat relieved that Day had at least seen the same phantom, he decided to take a holiday.

A couple of nights later, Day and a new engineer named Nicholson met the ghost train again at the same spot on the tracks as they neared Dunmore. Everything happened as before: the oncoming train blew its whistle and its ghosts waved as they passed silently through the night.

Not long afterward, in early July, Day was assigned a yard job at the station, so a different fireman accompanied Nicholson on the trip to Dunmore. A few kilometres out of Medicine Hat, a train appeared on the track again, bearing down on them. Seconds later they crashed head-on at full speed. Nicholson and ten others were killed in a horrific collision. The engineer on the other train, now dead, as the fortune teller had predicted, was Bob Twohey...just back from vacation.

We all sat there listening with our mouths open. And Dorothy just loved it. She even came up with something a little weird about Medicine Hat's name.

She said it came from a battle that was fought between the Cree and Blackfoot long ago near the local part of the South Saskatchewan River. It was said that the Cree medicine man deserted them in fear as things got tense, and he lost his headdress in the water. When his people saw it floating in the river they believed it was a dark omen. They laid down their weapons and were killed by their enemies. From that day forward that place was called "Medicine Man Hat."

The guys loved the stories, but I didn't really appreciate all this spooky stuff, knowing what Dorothy and I knew—or what I was worried might be true. I really didn't want to be told that southeastern Alberta was a place of phantoms and bad omens.

We whizzed southeast. Outside our windows the long stretches of flat land continued. Occasionally we saw the edges of the badlands, like foothills, inching their way over towards the road.

Dorothy got us playing this game she loved. It's called "I wish I were..." and you each have to finish the sentence. Bomber said, "A T. rex!" Terry chose "Jackie Chan!" Rhett picked "Bruce Lee," and I said, very quietly, "Norris Newcombe, the kung fu king." That just cracked up everyone. Dorothy said she'd like to be the movie star Marilyn Monroe, which was kind of strange, her being dead and all that.

We travelled for nearly an hour and then turned straight east just before we came to the Trans-Canada Highway. In about twenty minutes we started seeing the signs for Dinosaur Provincial Park.

Once we got on the smaller road that led to the park we could kind of feel it approaching. We all started leaning forward in the van, peering out the front windows. It was weird; there was some sort of tension building. I didn't need a dream to tell me that something was going to happen here. I stood up and stared, waiting for my first glimpse of this legendary land. My heart started pounding. It was like drums were beating.

9

LAND OF FEAR

In the distance the ground seemed to kind of fall away and the Land of Oz was back on earth again. Big time.

Newcombe turned off at the lookout on the edge of the park so we could see the whole thing beneath us. It was absolutely awesome. We got out of the van and walked to the edge, just staring.

Stretching out before us, as far as the eye could see, was a world of badlands. If we had been set down there from some other planet, this is what we would have thought the whole earth was like. There were a million Horseshoe and Horsethief canyons out there. You could just walk out into this place and never be found again.

Newcombe was giving us some information, and even his whiny voice couldn't make it uninteresting.

"Legend has it that near this very spot a Blackfoot family raised a teepee of buffalo hide, right at the edge. They stayed for a short period and then left. No one knows why. Their people have always believed that this is both a bad and a beautiful land. To them, it is very spiritual."

Imagine living right on the edge of that! No wonder they'd left. It would be pretty intense.

"This seventy-three-square-kilometre park is the richest dinosaur-fossil resource in the world."

"Wow," said Rhett, and Rhett isn't given to a lot of wows.

It actually took Newcombe a while to drag us away from the lookout. On the walk out we saw a huge plaque on which park officials had engraved comments that people from all over the world had made: from the US, Europe, Asia, Africa, everywhere. But the one I liked best was from a Canadian. "The land itself," he wrote, "seems like the bones of the earth."

Five minutes later we were descending into the main part of the park. Our first stop would be at the Royal Tyrrell Museum's field station. A model of a triceratops stood outside, and inside there was a little museum, much smaller than the one in Drumheller. This place was just an information centre, with a ticket booth for bus rides into the Restricted Area of the park, where we were going. We would spend a few hours out there and then head to Calgary and the flight home.

We had a little tour of the field station and then went outdoors to hang out while we waited for the three o'clock bus. Slowly other tourists started gathering. For something to do, Bomb climbed up on the triceratops. Ophelia was on his case like an albertosaurus, and he had to get down. She seemed to have reverted to her old, charming self.

Dorothy hadn't said anything about the Reptile since we'd left Dinosaur Valley; she seemed to have almost forgotten him. We were now far away from any evidence of his presence, real or imagined. Dorothy had been to the park only one other time, and she was obviously looking forward to her first trip into the Restricted Area.

We all loved the sound of the "Restricted Area." It was as though we were going somewhere forbidden— we ignored the fact that we would be on a guided tour with a whole bunch of other tourists.

Soon the bus pulled up. Actually, it was a sort of minibus with an all-terrain look to it, for getting around on the rough ground of the badlands, I suppose. When the bus driver got out, Bomber started making eyes at the rest of us. We knew what he was thinking: she was, in his words, "a babe." This woman was probably twice his age and likely could have taken him on a hike that would have just about killed him, or arm-wrestled him into the ground, but that didn't matter to Bomb, she was still "a babe" to him—though I don't think he really knows what a babe is, anyway.

She was a young woman with medium-length blond hair, blue eyes, and skin tanned brown from the sun. She was wearing the dark-green sweater—with a badge on the shoulder—and the lighter green shorts of a park ranger, and a park cap. She seemed very knowledgeable and capable, the sort of person who made you feel relaxed about everything. Ophelia liked her right from the start. And Newcombe, well, he just loved her. I've never seen him ask so many questions or listen with such fascination.

Her name was Katie Currie, but she said that everyone called her KD and we should, too. She started out by asking us a lot of questions. She stood at the front of the bus with a microphone and asked where everyone was from. There were people from Japan, England, the US, and, of course, us. Terry spoke up and very carefully explained why we were there. He was good at stuff like that.

KD then told us that Dinosaur Provincial Park was a World Heritage Site because of its unbelievable number of dinosaur fossils, its stunning badlands, and also its large collection of rare cottonwood trees. To be frank, we could have cared less about the trees—the other two attractions were what we had come for.

She explained to us that long ago the area had been a "lush, warm, coastal lowland." There had been a huge body of water in Alberta called the Bearpaw Sea, and the humid environment had been perfect for many animals, among them the dinosaurs. She said that almost every known species of dinosaur from the Late Cretaceous period had been found here. She mentioned the T. rex, the albertosaurus, and the maiasaura, or "good mother lizard," a favourite of hers, and the only dinosaur with a feminine name.

Once we got into the Restricted Area, we would be welcome to pick up dinosaur fossils. She made it sound easy. Apparently, they were all over the place. All you had to do was know how to pick them out among the other rocks.

"First of all, they have a kind of pink colour. Wet the end of one of your fingers and press it against a rock that you think might be a fossil. If the rock falls off, you have nothing…if it sticks, you have a dinosaur fossil."

This was going to be amazing.

KD hung up the microphone and got behind the wheel. Off we went, down through the public area where there were picnic tables and campsites. The road we were on was specially marked for tourists to follow—it was paved with brick and painted yellow. But suddenly it ended. Ahead of us, behind a very high fence, was an area that looked deserted. A big sign read, "RESTRICTED AREA. NATURAL PRESERVE. NO ADMITTANCE TO GENERAL PUBLIC. STAY OUT. DANGER!"

Inside the bus we looked at each other and smiled.

"Anyone want to open the gate?" asked KD.

Bomber jumped up and ran to the front of the bus. In seconds he was outside handling the gate. We drove through and he closed it. But as he was about to get back on board, KD suddenly gunned the motor and sped off. The look on the Bomb's face was priceless. It just sort of fell all over. Then KD slammed on the brakes and backed up. Bomb smiled and looked a little embarrassed as he climbed up the steps and found his way back to us.

"Sorry," said our ranger, turning around to us and switching on her mike, "just a little trick. But actually I did it for a reason. You saw the look on this young man's face when I pretended to leave him behind? Well, he was right to be afraid. That was the correct response. I want all of you to stay close to the bus *at all times.* We will be getting out for a few strolls but I don't want *anyone* to *ever* be *anywhere* where they can't see me. Believe me, inside the closed gates of the Restricted Area of Dinosaur Provincial Park without a ranger or transportation is not a place anyone wants to find himself or herself. Let me tell you why."

She explained that we could get lost, very quickly. Though all the hills in these badlands are different, they have a tendency to start looking the same, especially if you are a little frightened and start wandering off in the wrong direction. Before you know it you're either going in the opposite way you think you are, or just moving around in big circles. And though it wasn't the hottest time of the year, it was hot enough. Temperatures could reach 48 degrees Celsius in the park. And there was no water, anywhere.

"We don't go onto this preserve to protect people from getting lost. So you have to take some responsibility yourselves. We don't want you to turn into a fossil." KD liked to joke. But the facts she kept laying on us were no joke at all.

She said that the cactus quills in this area were like needles—they could pierce the soles of even the best hiking boots. The sun could damage your skin in no time. And there were caves all around. She didn't explain what she meant by that, but it sounded a little scary. What was in those caves?

Then it got even scarier.

"We have all kinds of animals on the preserve. There are coyotes, bobcats, mule deer, cottontail rabbits, and porcupines. But we also have snakes. There are lots of harmless ones—garters and hognoses—but there are others that you don't want to mess with. We have bull snakes here, constrictors that squeeze the life out of animals. They are at least two metres long."

"Whoa!" said Bomber.

"And we have rattlesnakes."

"Rattlers," said Rhett under his breath.

"The prairie rattlesnake is venomous. It is a pit viper. If it bites you, you will die within twenty-four hours. The poison does evil things to your digestive tract. But it isn't the only thing with venom around here. We also have northern scorpions. If they sting you, report it immediately. And then there are the lovely ladies of our park, the black widow spiders. If they inject their venom into you, you will get the chills, nausea, and paralyzing stomach cramps...it's all downhill from there."

She paused and smiled. "So...we have deadly rattlesnakes, constrictors longer than you are, black widow spiders, scorpions, bobcats, and coyotes. We have caves, blistering heat, cacti like knives, no water, and a labyrinth of hills that stretches as far as the eye can see. Even searching for lost people with airplanes or helicopters is almost useless. It takes special pilots who sometimes aren't available for days and people are very difficult to spot from the air here anyway. Understand why you should stay close to the bus?"

We understood.

"And another thing. If, God forbid, you ever do get lost out here, look for the flag. There is a red flag on a hill right next to the field station, the highest hill in the park. It can be seen from everywhere in the Restricted Area. If you follow it, you can find your way out. But you won't be needing that...will you?" She smiled.

"No, we won't," snapped Bomb. What a card.

KD placed the mike back on its hook, got behind the wheel, and we rumbled and banged forward on a rough gravel road. Occasionally she would rev the motor and start going pretty fast. It was a bit like a carnival ride when she did that. The tourists loved it. She started pointing out all sorts of things. She said there were three levels of soil in these badlands—sandstone, mudstone, and ironstone—though there were many more layers of history. She said the rate of erosion on this land was the fastest in the world. And she used some big words (which Terry wrote down in the little notebook he always carries) when she was talking about the glaciers. And she called the badlands "time-independent landscapes." I only partly knew what that meant, but I loved it, very cool…"time-independent landscapes."

There were funny things, too. Some of the land formations out there actually looked like animals. There was something the rangers called "the turtle," another one that looked like an "elephant head," and best of all, "Fred the Camel," who came complete with a nearby pyramid. The hoodoos were incredible—they made the ones at Drumheller look like they were minor league. We saw millions of them, huge ones and small ones, new ones and old ones. There was the "lonesome hoodoo" sitting off by itself, the "hairdoos" that actually looked like they had Beatle haircuts, and ones that KD called "nudoos," which were naked hoodoos—ones whose caps had fallen off. But it wasn't until we were well into the Restricted Area that we came to my favourite formation. It freaked me right out.

It was really a whole area, like a mini-canyon in the preserve. On all sides of us, hills started rising up and we seemed to be sinking. The hills looked like buildings from some sort of magical kingdom. And when KD told us what the area was called, it made perfect sense. "This," she said quietly, looking up as if still amazed, "is the Valley of the Castles."

"Awesome," said Dorothy quietly. I knew why she liked it. It looked like some sort of world far away, like something you might see in a movie. And it was kind of spooky, too.

At one point I asked KD about the legend of the living dinosaurs.

"I've heard that, too, but you'll never see them." She laughed. "It's said that they'll only show themselves to bad people. The story goes that they hate the fact that their ancestors are remembered as monsters, so they hide themselves. Dinosaurs only killed to survive, not to be evil, but we seem to really like the flesh-ripping side of them. I suppose that says something about us."

That made me feel a little guilty, and when I glanced at the guys, they were all kind of looking away.

"So," KD continued, "they won't show themselves to everyday folks." She laughed again. "At least, that's what they say!"

She let us out of the bus a couple of times at designated spots along the way. She showed us a bone bed that had been preserved and covered by a glassed-in case, another in a small building, and we had a great time finding fossils. What she had told us was absolutely right; they were everywhere, and if you licked your finger you could pick them up. They just stuck to you like glue. Me and the guys found tonnes.

We could see the places where the snakes gathered to lie in the sun, and when we climbed up several of the little hills and looked off into the distance, we could see badlands that just went on forever. It was getting very hot. A couple of times I asked Dorothy for a drink from her canteen. She let me, but she was very careful about it. I would barely get my lips to it and she'd pull it back.

Every time we stopped we stuck close to the bus. Once I looked up to see that red flag, high on the hill near the field station.

Little did I know that very soon I would search the skies for it…in absolute desperation.

10

LOST

Our ranger had told us that there would be just one more stop, and it would be at the farthest point the bus would go into the badlands. When we got out we were in a little opening among a series of steep hills that encircled us—supposedly a very good place for fossils.

Dorothy seemed to have totally forgotten about the Reptile by then and was getting more and more adventurous with each stop. She had barely been out of the bus for a minute when she ran up to the top of a hill and challenged the rest of us to try it, too. We did, of course. You can't let a girl beat you doing something like that.

So we were standing near the top of this hill. When we looked in one direction we could see the tour group, and in the other direction was this almost sheer drop. A few steps farther would have put us onto a thin, narrow piece of rock that jutted way out over the canyon, a hanging ledge. It looked dangerous. But suddenly, Dorothy ran onto it and stood there glaring back at us.

"Queen of the castle!" she shouted.

We piled up after her.

And that's when it happened. The whole thing just collapsed. Dorothy didn't scream because she wasn't the type to do that. And we didn't, of course, because we just couldn't. But we should have—maybe somebody would have heard us. Instead, we just fell. And fell. We rolled down the side of this mini-mountain in a five-kid avalanche, picking up speed as we went, like snowballs out of control. It seemed like an hour before we came to the bottom.

Bruised and battered, we got to our feet and looked up. We couldn't believe it. We were at the bottom of a mountainous cliff and there was no one in sight. We couldn't hear anything. Not even the wind.

"Uh-oh," said Terry.

At first we tried to climb back up, but that was useless. Then we resorted to yelling, but no one came.

So we made a decision, the dumbest of the whole trip. We decided to take a different route back to the top of the hill. It would be a long way, and we'd have to start out in a direction almost the opposite of the one we had come from. But if we went that way we could get to another hill that looked easy to climb, and from there we could double back towards our group. We started running. Before long we were sweating like pigs (and that includes Dorothy), and we were all out of breath.

When we got to the place we had seen from the bottom of the cliff, and looked back, we were surprised to discover that it was very hard to tell exactly where we were.

"This way," gasped Bomber, pointing to his left.

"Not a chance," said Rhett. "It's this direction." He pointed the opposite way.

I was confused, Dorothy was unsure, and Terry thought a third direction was right. We went with Rhett's idea. He just has a way about him that makes you want to do what he thinks is best. It's the way he is when he's killing a penalty and everybody else is nervous and freaking out.

Half an hour passed and we still hadn't found the hill. An hour later we were lost.

It's hard to describe the emotions that were going through me. I guess, all together, they would make up what people call a "sinking feeling." I was one part terrified, another part worried, and another part ready to cry.

You could see that Bomber and Terry were feeling the same way, but Dorothy and Rhett both had these calm, determined looks on their faces, as though they were going to solve this disaster. We kept walking, hoping something familiar would turn up. But finally we all stopped and sat down. At first no one said anything. We just kind of looked at each other. I glanced at my watch. We had been lost for *three hours!*

The ranger would have searched for us for a long time, but by now she would have taken the bus back to the field station. She would have alerted other rangers, and maybe even the RCMP, and a search party would be getting ready. Newcombe had to be just going nuts, and Ophelia…she would have fainted about a hundred more times. Thinking about her fainting didn't seem funny any more.

I was starting to really panic. I was wondering what would happen to us, and what the parental units would do when they heard. My mother always kidded me about things, and lately she was pretending not to be such a typical mom around me, because I was getting older, I guess, but she still got in just as many hugs and kisses as before. My dad's mind was always in the clouds, thinking about some case he was working on or some vacation adventure he was planning, but when he was doing something really exciting, he could hardly wait to tell me. They weren't nearly as bad as I usually said they were. I missed home. This would kill them. I'm their only kid.

I glanced around at the other guys. Dorothy still seemed okay, but Rhett was beginning to look as depressed as the rest of us.

This was actually happening to us. We were lost in the middle of nowhere, it was blazing hot, we had no food, and our only water was what was left in Dorothy's canteen. I felt a cry coming on again. So I stood up. I had to say something. First, because it would prevent me from blubbering, and second, because we needed a plan.

"So," I said as calmly as I could, my voice holding on, "what are we going to do?"

Bomber rose to his feet. He started to pace. "I don't know. I'm not the one with the brain. That's your job, Terry. If I had your smarts, I'd have us out of here in no time."

But Terry was silent. Our fearless goaltender was sitting with his head down and his hands were shaking.

"I'm afraid," he said quietly. "I don't have the guts for this. I can face a million pucks coming at me but I don't want to be lost in this place. I'm too scared to think." I heard him sniffle. "Rhett?" Surely Rhett, Mr. Cool, would have an idea.

"We'll be all right, Dylan," he replied without even thinking. "No problem."

"No problem!" I shouted. "What are you talking about, Norton?"

"I don't know, Maples, I'm just not the emotional sort! I'm trying not to freak out here. Maybe if I was all emotional like you seem to be, I'd come up with something. But I can't. Okay? Why don't you ask Osborne…And I need a drink of that water…NOW!" Dorothy hadn't been allowing anyone to drink from her canteen. She said we needed to preserve what we had for as long as we could. But Rhett wasn't just mad about that. He had never forgiven her for the things she had said to him back at the museum. He was funny that way. He acted cool, but he held grudges, took things personally.

Dorothy didn't even respond to him. The canteen stayed strapped over her shoulder. Instead she kind of leapt to her feet and tried to smile. "Why don't we just look at this as an adventure?" she said.

We couldn't believe it.

"An ADVENTURE?" cried Rhett.

She started walking as she talked. "Don't tell me I'm being unrealistic again! What else can we do? It is *very* important that we keep a positive outlook. If we panic, if we are frightened out of our minds, WE WILL DIE!"

Her voice echoed around the hills. She stopped for a moment, then continued.

"I'm just as afraid as the rest of you, and I don't have some perfect plan, but we have to get it together here. Besides, I've spent my whole life in Drumheller without anything exciting to do, and today I have something. This is life-and-death. I'm going to make the best of it. Now...think for a second, you guys, and let's come up with a plan."

There was silence. We were all staring at each other.

"Well, we can look for the flag," I said quietly.

We had been so freaked out that we hadn't even thought of the simplest solution to our problem: find the flag. I guess we had all felt, at first, that our sense of direction would eventually lead us back to the tour bus, but now we knew we couldn't trust our instincts in a badlands desert for a minute.

"Let's see," I continued, "when we were looking at it in the late afternoon the sun was kind of getting in my eyes, so that means..."

"The flag was in the west," said Terry.

"Right!" exclaimed Rhett, still sounding emotional.

"You're right, Bomber," said Dorothy.

"But...it's still a good idea to try to find the flag—we just won't know exactly where to look."

We all got up and started checking out the horizon. We spun around in every direction. No flag. But how could that be? Hadn't KD said that you could see it from everywhere?

"We must be really, really lost," said Rhett, sounding frightened again.

Our other problem was even scarier. In about half an hour we wouldn't even be able to see the flag if we were looking straight at it. It was getting dark.

"We have to get to higher ground," said Dorothy.

There was a hill not too far away that all of us were sure was higher than most of the others we could see. We started out towards it. But trying to reach it seemed like a bad dream. The more we walked, the farther away it seemed to get. Slowly the sun began to set.

"We have to stop," said Dorothy. "We have to find a place to sleep tonight and try our luck in the morning."

As frightening as that sounded, she was right. Human beings are useless in the dark.

We had passed quite a few caves during our walks, but no one wanted any part of them. Who knew what lurked inside? The best idea was to get down low somewhere so we would be sheltered from the wind if it picked up and wouldn't be easy prey for an animal. We wanted to be as hard to detect as possible.

Soon we found a place that seemed well protected, and we settled in. All of us were shaking by now and not trying to hide it. We were petrified out of our minds.

Dorothy tried to get us to play the "I wish I were…" game to get our thoughts off our fears. She went first and said "Somewhere else!" She tried to make a joke of it, but no one laughed. The answers got kind of weird. Terry said, very quietly, that he wished he were "brave"; Bomber said "smart," and Rhett said "emotional." I didn't know what to say, so I just whispered, "Something I'm not right now," and that ended the game. We all grew silent and kind of huddled near each other, and had a little drink of our water. I heard someone sniffling and thought of the parental units again. I wanted them near me in a way I hadn't since I was a little kid. This *had* to be one of my nightmares.

But it wasn't. It was so brutally real that I couldn't even sleep. It was deathly silent in the badlands at night, and I lay there listening. Then I heard a coyote howl and some sort of a growl...a bobcat? Suddenly, I felt something crawling on me. *No!* I leapt to my feet, quivering, and shook at it, jumping up and down and shrieking.

"Sorry," said Rhett. It had been his hand. He had reached out and put it on my shoulder. I couldn't believe that he, of all people, needed comfort. We were all feeling pretty freaked.

I lay down again. After a while I heard louder breathing and knew the others had somehow gone to sleep. I felt alone in the middle of the badlands. Mom and Dad always talked about the beauty of nature, and here I was out in one of the most stunning parts of our country...and absolutely terrified by it. It just didn't seem beautiful now. I remembered that when we were in Horsethief Canyon I'd thought that trekking way into that dangerous terrain and even getting lost would have been thrilling. That seemed incredibly stupid now. I sat there with my eyes open, not seeing very much in the darkness, just the outlines of those evil hills. Once or twice I thought I heard footsteps, and then a crawling sound, and a hiss. But it was all in my mind.

I lay there for what seemed like hours. Then, still unable to sleep, I sat up. Far off in the distance, I thought I saw something. I stood up and walked a couple of steps towards it. It was a light! And it seemed to flicker like a flame.

But then I started getting realistic. What could we do about it now? If we got up and walked towards it we would soon be even more lost, and who knew what we might stumble upon out there in that black wasteland? Cactus spikes through our shoes? Real black widow spiders crawling up our legs? There just had to be light to move.

I lay down again. *Who, or what, could have made that fire?* I finally drifted off to sleep, curled up and lying on my side, still trying to focus on that distant flicker until my eyelids became too heavy, despite all my worry and fear and desperation. A tear rolled down my cheek. For some reason, that light didn't comfort me. Did it mean hope…or danger?

Who was out there?

11

THE FLAG

IT WAS HORRIBLY DEPRESSING waking up the next morning. Several times in my life I've awakened in places I wasn't used to, and for a moment I didn't know where I was. Each time I panicked for an instant, felt totally at sea, but then got my bearings and was okay. I know that's a feeling everybody gets a few times in their lives. But I'd never felt anything like this. That first part, that panic, just kept right on going, for all of us, when we realized where we were.

It had been cold at night, and most of us woke up shivering. We started running sprints to get warm. Usually that sort of thing would have made us start goofing around. But there was none of that this time.

When we started slowing down, I remembered what I had seen in the night.

"I saw something when we were sleeping," I said to no one in particular.

"A fire?" asked Dorothy.

"Yeah," I replied, a little startled.

"Saw it too. This way?" She pointed off into the distance.

"That's right." I was surprised, and a little excited, to see that we agreed on the direction, too.

"A fire?" cried Rhett. "You guys saw a fire? Well, let's go!"

We headed out. We hadn't eaten since lunch the day before; I could feel my stomach rumbling. And soon it would get hot again. I knew the other guys were thinking about the same things, but no one said a word. We just walked steadily. The sun was in our eyes. There we no aircraft in the skies.

Dorothy moved up beside me.

"Uh, we seem to be going east. If we're still east of the field station, like we were on the tour, then we're going away from where we want to be."

"Right," I said, and paused. "But if someone did have a campfire out this way last night, our best bet is to go towards it, isn't it?"

"Probably."

I didn't ask her why she said that. I didn't want to know. We kept trudging along, and as we did I started to realize that we were looking for a needle in a haystack—everything looked the same again. But this seemed like the only hope we had. Dorothy and I were both convinced that we knew where we had seen the fire. And about twenty minutes later, much to our surprise, we found it.

It was a campfire, all right. But there was no one around. There weren't even footprints. Then Bomber found a clue. He was standing a few metres away on the other side of the still-smouldering fire and looking down.

"Whoever this is, he's alone. And he has a horse."

There were footprints all over the place. They came from a single horse. And whoever had been on it had cleverly covered up his own footprints before he mounted. Why would anyone do that? We followed the tracks for about ten or fifteen metres. The spaces between them began to widen.

"The horse is starting to move faster," said Dorothy, studying the prints. She walked several more paces, her eyes glued to the sand. "And here…it's galloping. This person left in a hurry and could be a long way off by now."

"Rats," said Terry.

I felt like saying more than that. Our spirits sank. We all sat around the dead fire and took another little drink of water. Only Bomber got up and wandered around.

A few minutes later, we heard him screaming. Our heads shot up and we leapt to our feet. We couldn't see him. He screamed again. It was blood-curdling. Racing off in the direction of his voice, we sprinted up a hill in no time and came down the other side. And there he was, pointing. And screaming.

"What?" I yelled. "Bomber! What?"

He turned around. He had a tear in his eye, but he didn't seem sad.

"The flag!" he shouted. "THE FLAG!"

We looked up. And there it was! The field station flag, high on a hill! I grabbed Dorothy and hugged her. She hugged back. Wrong move. We separated. Then I hugged Rhett. Even more wrong. We started slapping each other on the back and high-fiving instead.

"Let's head out, team!" I said. "Good adventure, Dorothy. But it's time to go home!"

There was a spring in our steps as we started off in the direction of the flag. It seemed as though it was pretty close, maybe about a forty-five-minute walk. And we would likely reach the edges of the Restricted

Area long before that. We goofed around as we walked and teased each other about who had been most afraid. Dorothy seemed more relieved than any of us, and she kept talking about what she was going to do when she got home. It was great to finally feel that horrible desperation evaporate. We celebrated by drinking the canteen almost dry.

But forty minutes later the flag didn't seem any closer. Well, at least we knew where we were going. It couldn't be long now.

It was. Another forty minutes of walking passed and we still weren't closer. It almost seemed as if the flag were moving. Then Dorothy, good old Dorothy, said something that put just a little of that desperation back into me.

"Notice anything strange about the flag?"

I looked at it, still so distant.

"No."

"It's, uh, in the east, too."

She was right. I didn't know what shape the Restricted Area was, but unless it sort of encircled the field station and we had doubled back and walked all the way around to the other side, then we seemed to be moving in the opposite direction from the way we should have been going.

"That *is* strange," was all I could say.

"Sure is," she mumbled.

"But look at it. That's the flag, all right. We *must* be going in the right direction."

"Must be," she said. But she didn't sound convinced.

Two hours later the heat was becoming unbearable, and the flag was still distant.

"We have to get out of the sun," groaned Bomber.

"Good idea," said Terry. "But where?"

I noticed Rhett wasn't saying much. In fact, he had hardly said anything all day. He seemed to be really struggling. His face looked white, and that worried me.

"What do you think, Rhetter?"

"Sure. Out of the sun."

That wasn't very encouraging.

There weren't any of those cottonwood trees around. In fact, there didn't seem to be really any shade of any sort. Except...I looked up high into the side of a hill. "We need to check out these caves."

"Caves?" said Terry. "No way! You won't catch me dead in any of those."

"You may be dead, period, if we don't get out of the sun for a while," said Dorothy. "Let's just rest for an hour or so and then move out again. The field station can't be that far away now."

The slow climb up the hill towards the caves was filled with dread. There were a dozen or more in the area we were approaching, and it was hard to tell what had made them. Wind? Water erosion? An animal? A human being? We hadn't asked the ranger, and now we were about to find out the hard way.

Terry announced that, though he was probably more afraid of the caves than anyone else, someone had to go in first. He disappeared. We waited. And waited.

"Cool!"

"Terry?"

He popped back out.

"They aren't very deep. I think they're just made by wind erosion. And there doesn't seem to be anything living in them, at least not now."

We all went in, ducking our heads to enter. The temperature dropped dramatically the minute we got out of the sun. None of us was in the mood for exploring, so we just sat down and waited. Before long we were all asleep.

I guess it was the rattling that woke me up. I don't have any baby brothers or sisters, so that was an unfamiliar sound to me. As exhausted as I was, it didn't even occur to me that I shouldn't be hearing a baby rattle, or that it was impossible for one to be shaking right near my ear when I was lost in the middle of Dinosaur Provincial Park. Slowly, reality began to dawn on me.

I opened my eyes. There was a hissing sound. *For real.* I leapt to my feet. My sleeping place was near the entrance, and no more than a metre away a prairie rattlesnake was making its way home...into our cave.

"Up! UP UP UP!" I shouted to the others.

"Dylan, go to sleep," said Bomber.

"SNAKE!" I shouted. "SNAKE!"

I've never seen any of them move faster than that. Not even for the free chips and pop after our hockey games. They were up in a flash. We flattened ourselves against a wall and slid by the snake and back into the sun. Outside there were dozens of rattlesnakes baking in the heat ten metres from the cave entrance! We flashed down the hill in an instant. At the bottom we bent over, hands on our knees, breathing hard. All of us except Dorothy.

She was trudging slowly down the hill behind us.

"They aren't apt to bite you, you know. Just stay clear of them and you're fine. The worst thing you can do is startle them by, uh...running...and screaming."

We ignored that.

"Let's get moving," I said. "We have to get to that flag before sunset."

But we didn't. We walked and walked. We grew so tired that we could hardly stand. And the flag just seemed to stay the same distance away. We couldn't believe it.

The sun was getting low, casting an orange glow over the sands. Unable to move any more, and too tired to make decisions, we slumped to the ground. I rolled over on my side and curled up. My eyes were wide open like a wooden dummy's and staring off into the distance, not registering anything. That's why I didn't clue in to what I was seeing at first. It was just a figure on the horizon. I was thinking about Mom and Dad, about my house and my room. All we had done was make a model of a dinosaur. And look where we had ended up.

Slowly that figure came into focus. I realized that Dorothy, who was right beside me, had sat up and was staring at the same thing. Though it was far away we could tell that it was a man standing on the edge of a cliff in the direction we had been walking. He was tall. Very tall. He was wearing a big black Stetson.

And he had the flag in his hand.

12

HUNTING HIM

W HEN WE HAD TALKED ABOUT the Reptile back at the Jurassic
Inn in Drumheller, Terry had said that if there
was going to be any hunting, then we would be the
prey. Well, now we were. He had led us deep into the
Restricted Area and had us exactly where he wanted
us. God only knew how far away from the field station
we were. Every step we had taken in pursuit of that
flag had taken us farther away from rescue and closer
to whatever he had planned for us. It was as if he had
just given us a signal. Now, he was going to hunt us
down.

Dorothy and I didn't have to hide the Reptile's presence from any of the guys. As we stared at him, terrified, we could sense that Rhett, Bomber, and Terry were looking, too.

"Oh, God," said Rhett.

God didn't have anything to do with it, near as I could tell. Satan was more like it. The Devil had come to southern Alberta and he was after us. *Why* was another question, one I didn't care to think about.

It took us a long time to start talking. By then the sun had completely gone down and the Reptile had disappeared. I heard a little bit of sniffling but I didn't ask any questions. I'd had a few moments of terror myself since I'd seen him, and I'd had to wipe away tears. Thank goodness it was dark out.

"Well." Dorothy's voice came out of nowhere, breaking the long silence. "Are we just going to lie here and let him come and get us?"

"No, let's go and take him on in hand-to-hand combat...you twit," shot back Rhett. He was tired, frightened, and angry.

"We're sure in the movies now," said Terry, his voice breaking.

But I figured Dorothy was right. We could either lie there like whimpering babies or do something. Maybe that something wouldn't be good enough, but at least we could try. In the video games at the museum, the T. rex didn't always win, and it must have been like that in real life, long ago in these badlands. But any time the prey actually got away, it was because it did something smart.

I imagined a meat-eater coming after a triceratops or an ankylosaurus right here in this valley seventy-five million years ago. I imagined the prey fighting back, desperate to live. Well, we were desperate all right, that part we had mastered. But how could we get away? How do you escape when someone twice your size and ten times as vicious has you in his sights?

"All right," I said, "count me in."

"The first thing we need to do is—" Dorothy started.

"Calm down," I said firmly.

She smiled. "Right."

"We could run, run as hard as we can go, but that would only tire us out, and he would likely catch us anyway."

"Right," said Dorothy again, "we need to find some other way to evade him."

"But first we need to sleep," said Bomber.

"Eh?" I said.

"He's not going after us in the dark. Not from that distance. And he is likely counting on us being tired and very afraid and desperate. Desperate enough to do something stupid. But we *won't* do anything stupid, will we? We will get some sleep, and in the morning we will make a plan. All we need to do right now is maintain a lookout."

"You know," said Dorothy, "you're not such an idiot after all, Connors."

"Thanks, Osborne…I think."

And so, right after we had seen probably the most terrifying vision in our lives…we slept. Each of us was the lookout for about an hour and a half. Only Rhett seemed to have a difficult time with it. He still worried me.

THE NEXT MORNING WAS LIKE the one before. I woke in a fog, unable to figure out where I was, then felt stunned by the hunger in my belly and remembered everything and almost panicked. I wanted to run. And scream while I did it. But Dorothy looked calm, so I tried to be, too. I figured we were all fooling each other about not freaking out, but this time lying to ourselves seemed to make a lot of sense.

"Let's move while we talk," suggested Dorothy.

"And let's stick to the bottoms of the hills," added Terry, "that way he has the least chance of spotting us. The hills will hide us."

And so we started out, trying to come up with a plan as we did. The ideas started slowly and then came fast and furious. We actually did consider the merits of running for a while, but running with a purpose. It seemed to us that the field station must indeed be still to the west—that's why the Reptile was leading us the other way. So we could run as hard as possible westward. But that wasn't the smartest idea, as Bomber pointed out, because west was an awfully big direction. We had no idea *where* in the west the field station was— we might miss it by a kilometre or two. And besides, as Bomber also figured out, that was probably exactly what the Reptile wanted us to do. He had taken us a long distance away from where we needed to be, like a lion drawing a gazelle into running for its life or an eagle hoping that a little mammal will come out of its hole and make a dash. When we ran, he would swoop. That's what he wanted.

"He's counting on us being predictable."

"So, we need to be unpredictable," said Terry.

"That means moving towards him," commented Dorothy with a steady look.

If she had said that two days ago (in fact, she sort of had) we would have told her she was a quintuple idiot (in fact, we sort of had), but now that crazy idea was actually beginning to make sense.

"He's like an animal, and he wants us to behave like animals, too. We have to use our brains. We have to behave like human beings and outsmart him."

"And how do we do that? I'd say that's the question." I hated to sound like a downer but I had to be realistic. How could we outsmart a guy in a life-and-death hunt when that guy was an expert at it? This wasn't a game. This wasn't something we could afford to lose. If he won, we were dead...for real.

It was the Bomb who first made a concrete suggestion. What he said was really what Dorothy had been saying for a while, but he fleshed it out. And when he did, it made the decision for all of us.

"We need to see him. Up close and personal. Then we'll know what he really looks like and what he has and how we might take advantage of him. There's five of us, we're a herd, remember. Now, let's think about where he might be."

"We don't have to," said Terry. "We know where he is, or at least where he was a little while ago."

"So let's make ourselves visible." That was Dorothy, always one for bizarre suggestions. "If we want to see him again, I think we need to go somewhere where he can get a clear view of *us*. Remember, he's tracking us, planning some trap. Let's go up on a hill and just stay there until he shows somewhere to the east. Then, *we* will track *him*."

"I don't know," said Rhett. It was the first time he'd said anything during this discussion. It wasn't much of a contribution, but at least he had spoken.

"No," I said, feeling a little energy, "it's perfect! Once we spot him, we might be able to stay out of his sightline and then watch him try to watch us. As he comes towards us…we'll come towards him. We must *always* know where he is."

"Then what will we do?"

"I don't know," I said. And I really didn't. What *would* we do once we got right up to this cold-blooded killer? What would we feel when we looked into his eyes?

Maybe we would just collapse in terror and he would kill us, one after the other. Or maybe we wouldn't even get that close. None of us was saying it, but in the backs of our minds we were all wondering if those tracks we had seen belonged to a horse that the Reptile was riding.

What chance would we stand then? We wouldn't even be able to run. Or what if he had a weapon? A gun? We didn't even want to consider that.

So we set off, looking for the tallest hill we could find, hoping to expose ourselves to one of the most feared villains in all of Canada. We were going to have to figure out the rest as we went along.

13

UP CLOSE AND PERSONAL

We picked our hill and up we went, like old-time criminals climbing a scaffold to meet the executioner. At the top we stood as tall as we could and scanned the horizon, mostly looking towards the east. We took out the canteen and drank the last few drops. Then we waited, our hearts pounding.

Sure enough, in about ten minutes he appeared. It was chilling to see his figure again, tall and black on the horizon. He didn't have the flag any more, didn't need it. It had done its job. He was still on a high, distant elevation. We saw him stop and then descend, quickly.

"Let's go! Let's do the hiding part!" snapped Rhett.

"No," said Terry, "this is where we do the whites-of-his-eyes thing. We need to see just exactly how he plans to get here."

Sure enough, we could follow his progress. We stood there for about ten minutes, watching him come all the way down to the bottom of the cliff he had been on. Then he began moving towards us.

"Look," cried Bomber. "Look what he's doing!"

"He's following that old riverbed," exclaimed Terry. "It goes…" His eyes followed a path that led towards us. "It goes right past us! That's how he's coming! All the way!"

I could feel the goosebumps come out on my skin.

"And he won't veer off," said Dorothy quietly, her eyes narrowing. "He will never even consider the idea that *we* might come after *him*. He'll just stay on that riverbed until he gets here."

"Let's go," I said.

And we were off. We headed down the hill, out of his sight, and then moved on a line that ran right in the direction he was coming from, but a few hundred metres off to the side, parallel to him.

Fifteen minutes later we stopped, and Terry scrambled up a hill to look for the Reptile. He came back down breathless. The big lizard was coming all right, moving at top speed, half a kilometre away!

We all sat down. It took us a few minutes to gather ourselves. I wanted to run again, and I could see the same fear in everyone else's eyes, especially Rhett's. Dorothy's look was kind of spooky, as though she had her mind on something she had been thinking about for a long time, just fixed on it, burning holes in it with her eyes. She looked frightened, too, but pumped, big time. "Do the unexpected," she whispered to herself, as if in a trance.

We got up and walked towards the Reptile. When we figured we were very close, we all crawled up a hill and peered over the top.

There he was!

So near I probably could have fired a puck that would have rolled right up to his boots. He was standing about as far away as one end of a rink is from the other. And he didn't look happy.

He stood still. Very still. He seemed to be listening. And he sniffed the air like a bloodhound tracking a scent. Then his head tilted on his shoulders like a bird's. He looked in front, to one side, then the other, then he turned and looked back in the direction from which he had come.

I had never seen a face like his. His eyes were like flattened diamonds, cat's eyes set far apart on a tall, thin head. His mouth was a slit. His skin, very white despite the sand and the sun, looked tough and wrinkled like leather. His whole face seemed as if it had been stretched over a skull, as if you could kind of see through to the bone. He was wearing a long black coat that hung almost to the ground and big black cowboy boots. That dark Stetson seemed a metre high on his head.

He scowled.

Then he turned and looked right at us.

Or, at least, it seemed like he did. But after a second he turned away, glancing in another direction. Finally, he started walking again, at the same frantic pace he had used when he came down the cliff and up the riverbed: big, wide ostrich strides. He was heading straight west, away from us.

"Whew!" said Rhett.

"We're going after him," proclaimed Dorothy.

"What? We've given him the slip, like you said. Now let's get out of here!"

"Where? Back towards the east? Away from the field station?"

"Dorothy's right, Rhett," said Bomber. "Listen, remember in football when Coach Garland always told us: *'Don't give your opponent the sidelines'*? He wanted us to force them to the centre, to where the action is. Because in the centre of the field you have more help. Your teammates can help you make the tackles. We want the Reptile to head back towards our help. That means closer to the field station, not away from it. If we go the other way and he figures it out, we'll be even more vulnerable than now."

"We have to stay downwind from this guy," I said. "We have to always have him in front of us. If we ever lose sight of him again...we're history."

I hated putting it that way. But it was the truth.

So we started following the Reptile. We stayed a couple hundred metres away, always on the other side of hills. One of us would walk higher up and dart to the top every now and then to see exactly where he was. For the longest time he just kept walking, maintaining that frantic pace, heading straight west.

It must have taken more than half an hour for him to slow down, but finally he did. And then he stopped.

I was on the lookout. I raised my hand to the others down below and they all stood still. Then I motioned to them and they edged up the hill near me.

He was looking around again. He had taken off his hat and was scratching his leathery, shaved head with his long, spidery fingers.

"Notice where he is?" whispered Dorothy. She sounded anxious.

"What do you mean?" I asked.

"He's where *we* were when he saw us from the top of the cliff."

And so he was.

He squatted down and looked at the ground around him.

"Were we ever *exactly* there? Right where he's standing?" I asked Dorothy.

"Yes," she whispered again, *"exactly* there."

The Reptile seemed to smile. He glanced up into the hills nearby and then at the spot where we were crouching. We lowered our heads for a few seconds and then peeked out again. He was picking something out of his pocket. It looked like food. He kind of gnawed on it for a couple of minutes. He pulled a huge canteen out of another massive pocket and took a swig from it. It was twice the size of ours. Then he lay down and put his hat over his head to shield his eyes from the sun. He was very still for a long time.

"What's going on?" asked Rhett.

"Do you think he's fallen asleep?" whispered Terry.

No one answered. We had all dropped down out of view and were lying flat on our backs. There was silence for the longest time. When someone finally spoke it was Dorothy, and she sounded frightened out of her mind.

"He knows we're here," she said.

14

A KILLER ON OUR TRAIL

Well, it looked like that moment was about to happen. That moment I had thought about a while back. The one when we would come face to face with the Reptile and find out what we were made of.

I didn't doubt what Dorothy had said. I had felt it, too, about a split second before she opened her mouth. And she hadn't tried to hide it. She had said it loud enough for everyone to hear, like she was mesmerized or something. Our wonderful, fearless Dorothy was about to lose it.

And so was I, and Bomber, and Rhett, of course. The only one who seemed calm was Terry. But what happened next took the courage out of even our bespectacled, strangely collected goaltender.

First we heard a noise, a sort of scurrying sound, like something rushing along the sand. Something big. I peered up over the peak of the hill.

The Reptile was almost on top of us!

He was screaming up the hill, arms outstretched, his billowing coat making him look like a giant buzzard swooping in for the kill. He screeched as he ran and locked his eyes onto us. It was as if the Wicked Witch of the West was right in front of us…on steroids.

We spread out and streaked down the hill in a hundred directions, like those gazelles running from the lion. All except Rhett. He just lay there, petrified. The Reptile swooped in and pounced.

The rest of us had gone down into a valley and up the side of another hill before we realized that we had lost someone. For some reason we had converged near the top of that hill and noticed that our pursuer wasn't on our tail any more. We turned and looked back. The Reptile was standing over Rhett with one foot on his chest, looking out across the valley directly at us.

It was *that moment*, clear and simple. We looked at each other. Without saying a single word we made a decision. We started to scream, and with that scream we took off, Terry in the lead, back down the hill and straight at the Reptile. He looked more than a little surprised. His prey wasn't supposed to do this. But we were a herd of enraged plant-eaters.

The Reptile took his foot off Rhett and stepped back. As he did, our cool defenceman, who had been so uncool since the minute we'd realized we were lost, seemed to recover. He leapt to his feet and ran with an energy I'd never seen in him. The Reptile turned as if to chase him but then looked back at us, approaching at top speed. He hesitated.

When Rhett was far enough away we veered off, like the Snowbirds in formation; Dorothy and I going one way and the other guys, following Rhett, running the other. Again the Reptile hesitated. Then...he went for us.

"CASTLES!" Dorothy shouted as we tore back down the hill. I didn't know why she said that, and I didn't really care. She might have just been *totally* losing it now. Who wouldn't, with the Reptile breathing down your neck? He was after us like a heat-seeking missile. As we went through the valley and back up the other hill, he seemed to be gaining on us, a Big Unfriendly Giant making those ostrich strides again.

Dorothy had fallen behind a little, and as I glanced back, I saw that the Reptile had almost caught her. He was reaching out one of those big skeletal hands with its long fingernails…closer, closer, trying to grab the part of her dress that was flying out behind her. This was one time when it didn't help to dress like a girl.

I spotted a big pink rock coming up to my right. It was a fossil about the size of a fist, but I didn't take the time to lick my finger or check it out. I just picked it up, planted my feet, and fired a high, hard one down the hill towards the Reptile's head. I'm not a baseball player, but I can "sling the pill," as they say. It caught him on the forehead just above his right eye. He groaned, fell back, and rolled down the hill. Dorothy sprinted up to me. We glanced back. The Reptile seemed stunned. He was on all fours, trying to get up.

Several hundred metres away now, on the side of another hill, Terry, Bomber, and Rhett were reaching a peak and disappearing. Dorothy and I did the same. And when we were out of sight we did so many zigs and zags through valleys and hills and rock formations that we lost all track of which direction we were going. But we didn't care any more. We just wanted to lose our giant hunter.

It took us a long time to feel safe enough to slow down. And even then we walked quickly, still breathing hard.

"I knew there was something about him that didn't make sense!" said Dorothy suddenly. "Other than the obvious!"

"What's that?" I puffed.

"He doesn't have a horse!"

She was right. He was on foot. So...who made that campfire? And who rode off at top speed on horseback?

It seemed like there was someone else out there, maybe involved in this in some way. *Who* was another question.

Despite our fatigue, our hunger, and fear, we kept walking. We had no idea where the other guys were now, or how near the Reptile was. All we knew was that we couldn't see him any more. And it was very quiet. Not long ago I had said that if we ever lost sight of him, we'd be dead. Now, I could only hope that wasn't true.

"What did you yell back there?" I asked Dorothy. "Castles?"

"If we have any hope of meeting anywhere," she gasped, "it has to be at a landmark. We all know the Valley of the Castles is somewhere west of here. It's big and it can be spotted from a long way off. I hope they understood."

Finding it would take a lot of luck. But so would surviving.

We headed west. Of course, the best plan would have been to move as quickly as possible. But we had little energy left and trudged along very slowly. Soon we came to more caves. One of them seemed larger than the others, and as we approached it, we could see that it had something over its entrance that looked like a roof sticking out from the earth.

"This must be one of those old caves that people lived in!" I said.

"Yeah, but nobody would live here now."

We walked up to it and entered. Sure enough, it had a roof, an old corrugated piece of tin driven into the side of the hill just over the opening. Inside we found remnants of an old table and chairs. The table was sitting upright and was littered with crumbs, including some scattered oats and a single cube of sugar. They seemed to have been left there recently. That should have meant something to us, but we were too tired to even try to figure it out.

We got out Dorothy's canteen, and then realized it was empty. She threw it at a wall, like she wanted to smash it into a thousand pieces. We sat down—angry, scared, and feeling desperate. We couldn't last much longer. And we couldn't pause in the cave for long, either. If we did, either the Reptile, hunger, or thirst would catch up to us. It was early afternoon. We both knew we had to make something happen today. So we roused ourselves for one last push.

"Let's head straight west as far as we can and keep walking as fast as we can. We have to find those castles," I said, with as much energy as I could muster.

But hours later we were as lost as ever. A couple of times we thought we saw our castle valley, our Emerald City, but each time we were disappointed. There just seemed to be so many rock formations that looked like magic kingdoms now. The only good news was that we hadn't seen the Reptile. Or at least that seemed like good news. It was hard to tell what was good and bad now, who was chasing and who was hunting. I started drifting in and out of dreams as I walked. The hills began to look like other things—dinosaurs at first, but then people, like my lost friends, and even my mom and dad. Dorothy and I were barely staggering forward.

It was time to give up. I had nothing left and I didn't care any more. I just wanted to drop and stay there. I wanted to find a way to say goodbye to my parents… maybe I would hold my hand over my heart. I figured we should look for some place out there, like another cave, where at least our bodies wouldn't be found by the Reptile.

Soon it would be dark. In fact, the sun was almost directly in our eyes. Dorothy was still walking with her head up. I was trying to figure out how to tell her what I was thinking: that I wanted to give up. For some reason my brain couldn't get my mouth to even form the words, and my legs just kept moving me forward mechanically. Finally, I focused. But just as I was about to speak we started hearing the strangest thing.

Music.

At first it was distant, but then it grew louder. Though I wasn't sure I was *really* hearing it, I *did* recognize it. It was an old rock song, one Mom and Dad listened to all the time. Dad used to crank it up so loud I had to leave the house. It was kind of spooky and he loved it.

"The Doors, man!" he'd shout at me as I tried to ignore him. "This is by The Doors!" That was an old band he was really into...still. "RIDERS ON THE STORM!" he would shout. Then he would dance around a little (very, very embarrassing) and try to explain what the lyrics meant, and tell me that people used to take drugs and listen to this song (all the time reminding me never to take drugs). He also said that the guy who sang it was into that sort of thing and died a mysterious death, and many people believe he's still alive (of course, when I say "people," I mean

the parental units and their friends). But I had to admit that "Riders on the Storm" was quite a tune, even if it was from the twentieth century. It was like a song sung by a ghost and his band. It had this freaky organ and a deep bass, and the sound of rain falling and thunder, and that dead guy's voice, just crooning over it all, about dogs in need of bones and riders in storms.

What a weird way to die, I thought. Maybe this was some sort of message from the parental units. Or from God or something. Why couldn't I sign off to some rap music, or maybe a little hip-hop?

I was hoping that Dorothy was hearing it, too. She had come to a halt.

"Do you hear that?" she asked.

"Uh-huh."

Good.

"Pretty freaky, eh?"

"What are riders on the storm?"

"Uh, I think it sort of means everybody, good and bad, except we're ghosts."

We walked towards the music. A little farther along, horse tracks began appearing on the ground. We stopped and looked at each other. We couldn't believe it—everything was happening at once! At first, the hoofprints led directly towards the song. But when they veered off, in the opposite direction, we had a decision to make. Finally, we decided to stick with the music. It just seemed to make more sense—we could always go back and pick up the tracks if this didn't work out. We moved on. The music became louder as we approached a particularly high hill.

We climbed it.

As we neared the crest, the landscape below began to open up for us. It was not only perfect for this spooky music...it was our Emerald City. It sat there in the fading light of the hot day like some sort of fantasy, coloured red and purple by the setting sun. *The Valley of the Castles!*

We slumped to our knees and stared at it the way we might have gazed at a fireworks display.

There was still no sign of where the music was coming from, or of our friends. But we did see something just a touch unusual. It was down in the valley, no more than five hundred metres away.

A dinosaur!

It was standing there looking as calm as could be. It wasn't a model or a painting or a cardboard cut-out or even one of the tiny lost dinosaurs that legend said lived somewhere in these parts. It was a ten-tonne, twenty-metre-tall dinosaur...as real as the setting sun. A plant-eater. An apatosaurus. A terrible lizard.

The music kept playing. The dinosaur raised its head and lowered it. It turned its long, slender neck, blinked its enormous eyes, and took a bite out of a tree. I couldn't remember any trees being there when we first came through.

I am hallucinating, I told myself.

"I am hallucinating."

And now I'm hearing myself speak in a girl's voice while my mouth is perfectly shut.

Dorothy shoved me. "Did you hear what I said? I'm hallucinating."

"Did you say that?"

"No, Dylan, it was the other guy. Who do you think said it?"

"Then, you're *not* hallucinating...and neither am I."

"But there's a ten-tonne dinosaur down there, munching on a tree."

"That's right."

"Oh, wow," she said softly.

We moved up to stand at the very peak of the hill. What we saw next chilled us.

There was a man, standing not far away, between the dinosaur and us. With each step a new part of him came into view. First, his black Stetson, then his white face, then his black coat and seven-foot-long frame. He was grinning from ear to ear.

"Riders on the Storm" grew louder. The thunder crashed, the organ played its eerie notes. The Reptile was singing along.

15

THE SHOWDOWN

Adrenaline is a funny thing. It can jump-start your body-engine even if you have no gas. It flowed through me now like Niagara Falls.

We turned and ran, splitting up again, this time totally on our own. I glanced back to see what the Reptile had done. One part of me wanted him to go for Dorothy; the other hoped he wouldn't. His head was snapping back and forth between the two of us. Then he made his decision.

He was after me!

I tore down the hill and did a sharp right turn. I had about a fifty-metre head start and I would need it. My plan was to go for that dinosaur. Plant-eater or not, it looked like help. It occurred to me, as I ran, that the Reptile hadn't seemed surprised that there was a seventy-five-million-year-old beast the size of an oil tanker just standing around in the sand behind him. Maybe the Reptile knew something about it. Maybe he would tell me before he killed me.

I glanced back again. He was gaining on me.

As I finished my wide turn and came back up the hill at a different angle, the apatosaurus came into view again. And so did Dorothy. She was heading for it, too. I didn't care now that we were going in the same direction. And neither did the Reptile. The three of us were in a straight line.

We hit lower ground and then it flattened out. I had to jump and twist and do all sorts of manoeuvres to get over the rough terrain, the dry riverbeds, and past the hoodoos, sitting there like ancient pillars.

The music grew louder. I gained on Dorothy. The Reptile gained on me. He started shouting and groaning. He seemed anxious to get to us before we got to the dinosaur.

Curiously, the apatosaurus didn't turn to see us. Its head just kept going up and down, sort of rhythmically. Were we just too small to see? I wracked my brain to try to remember…were dinosaurs hard of hearing?

Soon I could almost touch Dorothy. Her arms were pumping at her sides, I could see the sweat on the back of her neck, and she was puffing like a steer. When I reached her she didn't even turn to look at me. She just kept running, her eyes locked on that dinosaur. As we drew nearer, its size became absolutely awesome. I couldn't believe there had ever been an animal like this. It was a whole building on feet.

But the dinosaur still didn't look at us. Maybe it was the music, now so loud that we didn't even bother to yell to each other. Where was it coming from?

I couldn't hear the Reptile but I could feel him, within metres of us, reaching out. I arched my back and stretched my head forward, like a sprinter straining for the finishing line.

"Ahhhhhh!"

It was a high-pitched scream—from a girl. Dorothy was crying out like someone had shot her. And I could sense that she wasn't running any more. I stopped and turned around. About twenty metres behind me, the Reptile had her by the neck, one huge hand just wrapped around it from behind the way someone might grasp a chicken. And he was squeezing. She looked at me, terrified.

He glared.

What was I to do? Should I yell? Would the dinosaur respond? Weren't we still too far away? Or should I just run? The Reptile couldn't chase both of us at once. I could be free. I could go for help.

I hesitated.

Those eyes kept glaring at me. I could see the swelling over his right eye where I had nailed him with the rock. He raised his free hand and extended his index finger and beckoned for me to come to him.

No way.

I started to turn in the opposite direction.

"AHHHHHHHH!"

The Reptile squeezed Dorothy's neck like he was going to crush it in one hand. "STOP!" I shrieked.

He loosened his grip on her.

I walked slowly towards him, my shoulders slouching, my hands hanging down at my sides. When I reached the place where he was standing, his free hand snaked out and grabbed me, gripping me by the neck, too. He paused for a second, like a predator standing proudly over his prey. And then he started moving in the opposite direction from the dinosaur, almost dragging us along the sand. We didn't say anything. And neither did he. We were exhausted, starving, and beaten. I barely even cared where he was taking us. I just wanted this to end.

Five minutes later, he pulled us up a hill. He was heading towards a cave.

16

THE EVIL ONE

IT WAS THE BIGGEST OF ALL THE CAVES we had seen. He dragged us a few steps inside and then threw us onto the ground. We lay there for a few seconds and then lifted our heads. We weren't alone. Farther back in the cave, where it started to get dark, Rhett, Bomber, and Terry sat against a wall, looking grim. Their hands and feet were tied.

But none of us said anything. Our captor did all the talking.

"Welcome to the Reptile's nest," he hissed, walking as he spoke, never straying more than a leap from the entrance. "This is where it gets exciting; where it gets *real*. Let's just say, you're not in Drumheller any more."

Each time he came near me, I flattened myself against the wall in fear. My mind was racing. I couldn't believe he had us. *We were going to die.*

I hadn't really looked very closely at Rhett, Bomber, and Terry at first. Now I did. They glanced back in fear. They all seemed weak, and their eyes were blood red.

"I'm sure you're all dinosaur fans," continued the Reptile, his deep voice echoing in the cave. "Like to see them ripping each other apart, no doubt. Well, I'm a bit like those beasts you admire. Think of me as the new albertosaurus." He chomped his teeth at us.

Suddenly those video games we all loved seemed pretty awful. Near me, Dorothy was starting to cry, which I couldn't believe. "I want to go home," she said quietly.

The Reptile heard her.

"Home? To dreary Drumheller?" he barked at her. "And miss all this excitement?"

"I want to go home," said Dorothy again. "Why were you following us? What are you going to do to us?"

"Following you?" He seemed surprised. "I wasn't following you. I came from Drumheller along the same route, no doubt, but if you think I was following you, then you were imagining things. I was just trying to get away. Once you were lost here, though, I realized that I could *use* you. You were young, vulnerable prey, cut from the main herd. But frankly, I'm still just doing what I need to do to survive. I will only harm you if you get in my way. So far you've done what I require. I drew you to me, and here you are.

"You see, the world thinks I kill children, but I have never harmed a child in my life. Murdered someone who picked me up by the side of a highway, true, but these things happen. Passion and love sometimes turn to violence. Unavoidable." He smiled.

Smiles aren't supposed to make you feel like your life is about to end. But this one did.

"I *could* harm a child, of course, if that were necessary. But accusations linking me to children's deaths in the past are preposterous. They needed a suspect when the fools couldn't solve certain crimes, and I was convenient. After all, I like to dress the part—all in black with the matching Stetson. That's how I looked at my court appearance, useless as it was. I am rather tall, though not seven feet, as they say. I like to wear my hair rather short, am prone to a little drama, and admit to my crime—though I don't believe I deserve all my sentence. And these children who were murdered—the diseased person who did it had a thing for human bones. So do I. What of it? They seem to think there is some similarity.

I am a perfect suspect for them to demonize. They have a prejudice about me. But it's a good thing, in a way. For me, it's best to be feared. When a bone is found lying around in my wake, it creates a certain edge. So I found that bone and left it not far from the museum. It was meant to keep their focus on Drumheller, as was my appearance at Horsethief Canyon. All in preparation for my flight here. It seems to have worked."

He walked over to me and squatted down, staring straight into my eyes. My heart started pounding so fast I thought it would break my ribs.

"They will likely track me here before long. And you, my little ones, are my insurance policy, perfect protection. You see, if they think I will murder you," he whispered, "if they think you are in mortal danger, then so much the better for me. I want them to pursue *you*, not me. There is only one way to get them off the Reptile's scent. Children! You will be their priority. Out in a desert like this I can get away if I have a diversion. You are like a gift to me. You will help me escape... forever."

He stood up and walked towards the guys. Reaching down, he put his hands on Rhett, who froze. The others cringed. But the Reptile just sighed. Then he untied each one of them.

"I will let these three go...because I am so caring and loving." He turned towards Dorothy and me and lowered his voice. *"Then I will take you two with me for protection and head east."* He obviously didn't want the guys to hear his plans, but maybe he'd spoken too loudly. I glanced at Bomber and our eyes met.

The Reptile's head snapped sharply towards the three of them and he stepped away from the entrance. "Be off with you!" he said.

They struggled to their feet and walked as quickly as they could. Terry took the lead.

Near the entrance the Reptile shoved them out. "Move straight out from here. You'll run into some company soon. And don't try to follow us or have us followed, or it will mean death to your friends!"

The guys glanced over at us, scared, unsure, and then vanished into the night. I kept my eyes on Bomber. Had he heard what the Reptile said?

There was silence after they left. Our big captor just stood there watching them for a while.

"Fools," he finally said. "Do they really think I would tell them which way I am going?" My heart sank as he turned on us. "We will head northwest, back towards Drumheller. Halfway out I'll leave you two, hands tied and blindfolded, nowhere near shade or water. If your friends pass on the message to their rescuers—and they *will* be rescued, believe me—then everyone will search for me in the wrong direction. And when they figure out which way we really went, *if* they figure it out, then I will be long gone. Perhaps they will find this cave, the last place your friends saw you alive, and they will track us to the place I'll leave you, deep in the desert. But will you still be there? Or will you have wandered blindly in search of shade, in search of water, knowing that your life depends on it? They will be forced…morally…to devote much, or even all, of their manpower to following *your* tracks, not mine. It will kill their search, or weaken it, fatally. Save the children first, you see…. Suckers."

"Why are you doing this?" said Dorothy, just blurting it out. I couldn't believe she was trying to talk to the Reptile again. She seemed to have recovered a little. Her face looked defiant.

He twisted his long neck around and almost snarled at her. "I will do whatever I need to do to survive. That's what we all do."

"What about right and wrong?"

Oh man, why did she say that? Antagonize him, Dorothy, good idea. She really was like something from a movie. One for the kiddies. Who did she think she was, Anne of Green Gables?

"Right and wrong?" asked the Reptile with a smirk. "There is reality and there is fantasy, not right and wrong. No one cares about right and wrong any more. That's an old idea. Whatever happens happens, whatever works works. Life is a business now. I am a businessman of a sort. I am what I am."

"You aren't an animal."

"I am being hunted like one! Now, spare me the speeches they give in books, little girl." He had had enough. He waved us forward. "Let's move out. As long as you two keep up, this will be a breeze. No one knows we're here."

"No one?" I asked, before I could stop myself. I had suddenly remembered the hoofprints we had seen in the sand nearby.

"Of course not. No one is on to us, yet. And they won't be for at least a few hours."

A few hours? What was he talking about?

"How did you get here from Drumheller?" I asked, my mind racing.

"I had a horse, if you must know. I stole it from that saloon in Wayne."

"*Had* a horse?" I blurted out.

"I dumped it before I reached the park. I couldn't find enough water for the poor beast. You know, I was once a member of my local humane society. Let no one ever say that the Reptile is cruel to animals." For an instant, a smile flickered across his face. But it quickly faded. "No more questions. Let's move."

He reached down and lifted something off the ground. It looked like one of those lights people have on their ceilings, for track lighting. Except it was much bigger. It was more like a searchlight, the kind used to light a whole street on the set of a movie. They're always shooting movies in Toronto, so I'd seen lots of them. But what was it doing here? I could see it had a switch. It seemed as though it was battery operated.

"Once we get farther away from the cave, this will come in handy," he said. "Ah, showbiz."

Dorothy and I exchanged glances. I could tell by her expression that she had thought of the hoofprints, too. We had the same idea as we moved out into the darkness. *The horse. The searchlight.* Before long, we both started stumbling—on purpose.

"What's wrong with you?" snapped the Reptile. "Can't you two walk?"

"I can't see," said Dorothy. "We need some light."

"Forget it. Not until we get further into the park. Walk!"

But a few more minutes of our stumbling changed his mind. "All right," he said, "you can use the searchlight, on low. But just for a few minutes, until you're used to the footing." He thrust the light into my hands.

We were hoping that in minutes we would know all about that horse. Was it still in the area? Was it Grant Tyson's best horse, the stolen "John Ware" from Wayne? *Was someone new riding it? Or was there someone else out there?* I turned on the searchlight. Pretending to be awkward, I let it flash around on the hillsides, letting it linger a bit in the area where I figured we had seen the tracks. About ten minutes later we heard the sound of hooves.

The Reptile hissed at us. "Stop! And douse that light!" We all stood still in the darkness. The sound stopped. We looked up at the ghostly castles on the hillsides.

"Start moving!" said the Reptile in another agitated whisper. "And no one makes a sound!"

But when we moved, the hooves moved. Several times we stopped. Silence. Then we walked again. Horse's hooves. Finally, we stood still for a long time. The hooves started again and came towards us at a very slow pace. The Reptile turned towards the sound. A ghostly form began emerging from the darkness. What sort of beast would it be? First we saw the eyes, then a horse's head, then a body...and no rider. A saddle was strapped to its back. The saddle was marked with the scarlet and gold of the RCMP.

"Halt, Flame!" said a voice out of the darkness. It sounded familiar, and it was right behind us. A man grabbed us and pulled us back, shielding us with his body. He was wearing a white Stetson. We heard his pistol click into firing position. "I believe I have my man," said Steele Lougheed, training his firearm at that big, shaved head.

But the Reptile didn't come by his reputation for no reason. He instantly vanished into the darkness like a phantom, bolting away at top speed. Just as quickly Lougheed was after him.

"Stay with Flame!" he shouted. "He knows the way out."

We heard them run into the night. And before long we could hear nothing.

"Well," said Dorothy, "I'm not standing on the sidelines." She put one foot into the stirrup and threw herself onto Flame's back. "Give me that!" she cried, pointing at the searchlight. But I wasn't about to miss this either.

"Only if I come with it!" I shouted, putting the light in one hand, a foot onto a big rock beside the horse, and throwing myself up behind Dorothy into Lougheed's big saddle. I switched on the beam, Dorothy brought her heels into Flame's side, and we shot off like two human cannonballs into the night.

Bouncing up and down and barely holding on, I scanned all around with the light and soon saw them, running at full speed a couple hundred metres in front of us. Then we turned a corner in the Valley of the Castles and everything got weird. Very weird. *The whole far end of the valley was lit up with an otherworldly glow!* The hills, the valley, everything, gleamed like something from a dream. And right smack in the middle of that light, just standing there, perfectly still…was *the dinosaur*!

We came thundering towards the glowing scene. It grew brighter, like it was day instead of night. First came the Reptile, then Lougheed, and then us.

The music started again. The rain came down, the thunder crashed, the drums, the bass, and the guitar began, and that eerie electric piano cascaded over everything. The dinosaur started to move, its head almost bobbing in time to the second verse of "Riders on the Storm"; something about a killer on a road with a brain squirming like a toad, something about death too.

As we approached at top speed, we could see that *people* were gathered around the dinosaur now. A whole crew of people. There were many more lights like the kind we had with us, and boom microphones on long steel poles, and cameras, and cranes. A man in a red beret was shouting through a megaphone in an American accent.

"Okay, this is just before the T. rex rips apart the plant-eater! All right, people, I need this to be spooky and freaky! And real. *Real* real, *comprendez?* Music's good! Turn it up! *Dinosaur Wars II*, take fifteen! Cue the violence!"

The Reptile rushed on, closing in on the bright lights as we closed in on both him and Steele Lougheed. Off to our right, just emerging out the darkness, I could see Rhett, Terry, and Bomber staggering forward as fast as they could go, drawn by the lights.

I stared up at the dinosaur as we neared. It had a stunned look in its eyes. And the eyes didn't look like eyes at all. Then a sign came into view behind the man in the red beret. "*Dinosaur Wars II*, Scarecrow Productions, Hollywood, California" it read, in big, gold letters. That dinosaur was a massive, animatronic work of genius from the geniuses who can fake anything! Nearby I saw a big pile of "human" skeletons. Now I knew where our criminal wizard had found his mysterious bone—this crew had been in Drumheller when we first got there!

The Reptile arrived without warning, thundering onto the movie set. When he came into the cameras' view the director started to swear. The others looked stunned. But soon a man holding a script and a pen ran forward, squealing with delight.

"Wow!" he gushed. "Do you *see* this! He looks *dangerous! Very real!* We can USE THIS!"

The Reptile's face gleamed a lurid shade in the set's lights. His eyes glowed deep in his sockets. He turned and saw the film crew and glowered at them.

"Cameras rolling!" shouted the director suddenly, not swearing any more. And so, they filmed it. In came Lougheed at full speed, the lights shining off the buttons of his uniform.

"Oh man, a Mountie! This is to die for!" shouted the guy holding the script.

We cut across the set on the horse at full gallop, knocking things down as we went. We weren't quite as big a hit with the Hollywood guys.

"KIDS!" shrieked the director. "They're ruining everything! There's *no* place for kids in this!"

But we didn't hear much else from him because we were soon all gone from the set and back out into the night. The music swelled. Someone had cranked it up.

There was no way we were letting the Reptile get away. We just had to catch him. The film crew started to run after us, their Steadicam pointed straight into our search beam, looking for the Reptile and the Mountie. Suddenly there was a horrific scream. It sounded like our prey.

We moved forward a little, and so did the camera crew, searching with our light. We saw Lougheed, standing alone, his gun in his holster, breathing hard, frantically looking for the Reptile, just as we were.

Then we caught sight of him, kicking his feet at something, still screaming. Lougheed spotted him and moved in. In an instant he had him down and the handcuffs on. The Reptile stiffened. He wouldn't speak. He wouldn't say what had tormented him in the night. He almost seemed embarrassed.

NORRIS ARRIVED WITH OPHELIA about an hour later. The film crew had finally gotten a call through and the Newcombes were nearby in the town of Brooks. They were so excited to see us that I thought Norris himself was going to faint. He set down that briefcase of his, pulled out a container of bottled water about the size of a swimming-pool noodle, and started drinking and splashing his face so he would stay upright. I guess the whole thing had been pretty rough on both of them. They'd not only been devastated by our disappearance, but they'd had to explain everything to all our parents and to the school principal. Then the media had gotten hold of it and kind of cornered them in their hotel room. Norris looked as though he hadn't slept for about a decade, and Ophelia must have had a bucket of makeup on; I guess her poor face needed it.

All the parental units had flown in to Calgary on the second day we were lost and were on their way, making all sorts of demands about doctors checking us out and that sort of thing.

We were okay. Well, we were exhausted, hungry, dehydrated, and sunburned to the point where we each looked like a pizza on a stick. But really, we were all right. The doctors checked us out and pumped vitamins and fluids into us until we almost wished we could just go back out into the badlands.

When Mom and Dad got there, I had to admit to being relieved. They were what I really needed. Mom got in all the hugs she wanted. And Dad, he just kept slapping me on the back and saying stuff like, "Way to go, champ! Thought we'd lost you!" Then his eyes would get a little red and he'd walk away for a while. I'd never tell *them* this, but I was really looking forward to going back to Toronto with them to recover from all of this—there's really nothing a little love and home sweet home won't cure.

Actually, our biggest problem was Ophelia. The moment she saw us, she actually threw her arms around us and tried to kiss us!

And next morning something else happened that was nearly as revolting—Newcombe saw the Reptile being moved into a truck and immediately went into some sort of a stance. It looked disturbingly like a kung fu move. And he did it right in front of a whole battalion of Mounties. Gag me!

It was a pretty happy bus ride back to Drumheller, where we were all going to relax for a day. The parental units, the Nortons, the Singhs, and the Connorses, were in their rental cars right behind us, following us like mother bears or something. Rhett, who was just bouncing off the walls of the bus with happiness, started the "Wish I were…" game. "Myself!" shouted Dorothy, looking at us with a grin.

"Five kids," I cracked, "on their way home!" No one else could top that. And when we got to Drum, it seemed almost like home. I smiled at the dinosaurs on the sidewalks and the garbage cans shaped like hoodoos.

It had been a horrible few days. But Dorothy and I and my three friends had learned a lot about ourselves out in that strange land. I'd seen some new sides to old buddies. I'd always thought Bomber was the dim-bulb of the group, but he'd come up with some pretty smart ideas when we got lost; Terry, who was easily the most timid of the guys, actually displayed more courage out there than the rest of us at times; and Rhett, good old Rhett, who we all admired because he was so cool, had shown the least heart when it counted, and then the most emotion when everything turned out well. He was even hugging Dorothy at the end. I guess it goes to show that people aren't always exactly what they seem.

That night the parental units and I gathered around the supper table at the Osborne house and talked. Dorothy was acting a little funny—she was telling Mom and Dad what a fantastic place Drumheller was, and she really seemed to mean it! The food was great, heaped on our plates like the Rocky Mountains: roast beef and baked potatoes and buttered vegetables and lots of pie for dessert, a good old-fashioned western Canadian meal. Everything was perfect, except for the parental units, both pairs. Dad had heard about The Doors song and was going on and on about it with Dorothy's dad, who strangely didn't seem to mind a bit.

"It's about love being greater than evil!" exclaimed Dad.

"Girl, you've gotta love your man," sang Mom and Dorothy's mom in unison, finishing off the song. *"Take him by the hand, make him understand…the world on you depends!"*

"Gag me," whispered Dorothy. But she barely got it out because we were enveloped in a group hug by all four adults. I hate to admit it, but it felt pretty good. Being wrapped up in their arms with Dorothy was better than being chased by the Reptile any day, in any time, past or present.

AFTER DINNER DOROTHY TOLD ME she had something she wanted to show me. We headed off into a fairly dark room at the back of their house. It had a row of couches and big soft chairs and the largest big-screen television I'd ever seen.

"This is what we call the screening room," she said. "Sometimes Mom and Dad even show real movies here, using a film projector. Just like you'd see in the theatre. They have all the equipment."

She pulled something out from behind her back. "I have a surprise," she said. It was an old videocassette.

"A movie?"

"Sort of. It's part of one. *Dinosaur Wars II... Interrupted.*" She laughed. "It turns out the director of that movie wanted the part we ended up in to be shot on an old-fashioned videocam. But he was so upset with us appearing in it that he told the cameraman to just throw out all the tape he used that night. Said even the part with 'the freak' was useless. I, uh..."— she smiled—"took the liberty of picking it out of the garbage bin. Mom and Dad have an old VCR here."

A few minutes later we were watching the Reptile come snorting onto the screen, with a Mountie and two kids on horseback in pursuit. It was a very weird thing to look at. It wasn't like watching a movie, though. It was frightening and very real. We watched as we rode off into the night, and the picture started getting darker and unfocused as the cameraman chased after us, catching glimpses of the Reptile spotlighted in the darkness. Then there was a pause.

"That must be where he screamed," I said.

Dorothy had left the remote control on top of the television. She stood up to get it. The tape was about to end.

"Hold it!" I said. Before us on the large screen we could see dark images of the Reptile suddenly dancing in horror in front of us. It was very murky. He seemed to be kicking at something near his feet. Then the screen went blank.

"Can you run that back and slow it down?" I asked.

Dorothy rewound and we watched. When the Reptile started kicking, she put the tape on slow motion.

There, at his feet, small animals were attacking him. They looked like lizards. But they weren't like any lizards we had ever seen before. We froze it and walked up to the screen. They had long tails, stood upright on their legs, and had sharp teeth like razors. We saw bright, yellow eyes, on fire.

They were miniature dinosaurs! Prehistoric creatures. Alive!

"Dorothy, don't ever leave here," I said, stunned, my eyes riveted on the screen.

"Why?" she whispered.

"Because you live in the Land of Oz."

MORE DYLAN MAPLES ADVENTURES

The Mystery of
Ireland's Eye
978-1-77108-615-8

The Secret of
the Silver Mines
978-1-77108-703-2

Coming Soon:

Monster in the Mountains (April 2019)

Phantom of Fire (July 2019)

ABOUT THE AUTHOR

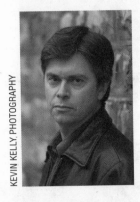

Shane Peacock is a novelist, playwright, journalist, and television screenwriter for audiences of all ages. Among his novels are *Last Message*, a contribution to the groundbreaking Seven Series for young readers, and The Dark Missions of Edgar Brim, a trilogy for teens. His picture book, *The Artist and Me*, was shortlisted for the Marilyn Baillie Award. His bestselling series for young adults, The Boy Sherlock Holmes, has been published in twelve languages and has found its way onto more than sixty shortlists. It won the prestigious Violet Downey Award, two Arthur Ellis Awards for crime fiction, the Ruth & Sylvia Schwartz Award, The Libris Award, and has been a finalist for the Governor General's Award and three times nominated for the TD Canadian Children's Literature Award; as well, each novel in the series was named a Junior Library Guild of America Premier Selection. Visit shanepeacock.ca.